Curse of the Ratman

Jay Wilburn

Madness Heart Press

Madness Heart Press
2006 Idlewilde Run Dr.
Austin, Texas 78744

First Edition
www.madnessheart.press

This is a bloody, gross story. Not the sort of thing I want to dedicate to respectable people in my life. So, I dedicate it to **Drew Stepek** and his vision of godless.com, without which this and a couple other of my most beloved and devious stories wouldn't have seen the light of day. And to **John Baltisberger**, who liked it enough to see it in print, allowing me to hold it in my hands and pass it on to others. That's a pretty big deal to me.

1

Rat shit dribbled from his empty sockets like tears. A ribbed tail flicked out of his drooping lips and licked the syrupy shit away, as deft as any man's tongue ever could.

And he was still a man. Fuck anyone that said he wasn't. He expected things like a man. He demanded respect like a man. He hated like a man. By whatever god had made him, he still hated as good as any damned man.

He watched with hollow eyes, across the Ironheel Creek, as they slept in their tents near the rising smoke of a dying fire. He could kill them all, as he had done others in the past, when they forced him to do it.

The river noise would cover his approach. Half of them would be ended before the others woke up from the screaming. Some would try to fight, while others tried to run, but they would all fail and they would all

4

die.

And he would feed. The things living inside him would feed, and he would grow.

He could grow much, much bigger than he already was.

It would be easier just to kill them all now, but they were here finally. They were here, and that might mean they had remembered their promises. He needed to wait at least that long, just to see.

He was a creature of broken promises, both in his life, and with what he had become since then. If they did not keep their promises, he had to kill and he had to feed.

And they would all have to pay, to the last child, to the last generation.

It was their responsibility and their burden to carry, for generations. This generation had seemed to have forgotten that.

But they were here now, so maybe it wasn't too late.

A squirt of urine spilled from one stretched-out nostril like a nosebleed. It was so yellow it almost glowed like toxic waste. He didn't move. Didn't acknowledge it. He sat there so long it dried, leaving a white, crumby crust of mineralized calcium.

Across the creek, one of them was moving. This one was a Rinder. He could smell it on the man, even from across the river. The realization inspired the things under his skin to scurry, causing his body to lose shape for a moment.

What happened now would decide everything.

There was still a little time left to make it right, but only a little.

He backed away from the creek and disappeared into the brush. From there, he would watch with hollow eyes and see what this generation of Rinders decided to do with their promises.

jay Wilburn

"Son, you need to wake up."

Tommy Rinder's head hurt, but he sat up in the dark. He could smell the mildew inside the canvas tent. He still had on his tan uniform shirt, clinging to him with stinging sweat, inside his sleeping bag. He had just turned thirteen years old and was still not entirely used to sleeping out in the woods.

This July, in the summer of 1979, was proving to be one of the hottest ever in the Carolinas. That was true here in the woods of North Carolina for this Boy Scout trip. It was true back home in Butler, South Carolina, ten miles inland from Fuller Beach, on the coast. Hot, muggy, and often windless both day and night. Heat lightning scratched the sky over and over with broken promises of cooling rain.

He did not remember falling asleep. That was bad.

The other boys would cut the hair or stick things in the mouth of the first one to fall asleep. Tommy reached up and felt all his hair still there. He tried not to think about how his mouth tasted.

He heard the familiar wood-sawing sound of snoring. It could have been one of the boys, but it sounded adult.

He lay his head back down on the fabric of his sleeping bag.

"Tommy."

He sat up and said, "Who the hell?"

A hand clapped over his mouth hard enough to feel like a slap, and stayed there. Tommy tasted dirt and smelled kerosene.

"Come out quietly, boy. Be sure you got your pants and hiking boots on."

Tommy felt a shrinking fear in his groin, but all he could think was that he had just said "hell" in front of his father. Back home, such a thing would have resulted in Tommy going to cut his own switch from the willow tree. His sisters would start betting how many lashes Tommy could take before he started crying.

Their father, Carter Rinder, was a prison guard out at Grinder State Prison, there in Rutledge County, South Carolina. He took no guff from inmates or kids when it came to respect or discipline. Although, Tommy thought his sisters got away with murder sometimes.

Out in the woods, with the women back home, sometimes the rules were different and the lines were greyed out into ashy smudges that smelled of smothered campfires. The men would still pop their boys upside the head for crying over a splinter, or for talking back to one of the assistant scout masters. In the waning years of the 1970s, men seldom popped another man's boy, like was acceptable in Tommy's father's stories of Boy Scouts from a generation earlier, but it sometimes happened for scratching a car or dumping a full pack of supplies in the river from slipping on a rock. Then, sometimes they just laughed about it, if their mood was smudgy in that moment.

A boy saying hell in the presence of his mother was a damnable offense, no matter what a boy's father might have said while working on a car. Out in the woods, the men told stories of bloody hooks in doors, and sometimes jokes about their peckers, where the boys could hear.

Tommy thought, *Tell your mother thanks. For what? For helping pull my log out between my two flat tires.*

His father clicked his tongue outside the tent flap. "Boy?"

Tommy yanked on his jeans instead of the green uniform pants they wore during travel days. He had trouble in the dark getting the thick laces into the metal hooks of his boots. He knew he missed a couple in the dark. He tied off the shoes anyway, hoping they weren't going far.

He could hear his father's clicking tongue from across a neighborhood. It always meant hurry. In church, it meant he was getting it as soon as Jesus was the only

10

one looking. This far up in the mountains, Tommy had no idea what it meant.

He pushed out of the tent, where his father stood dressed. The man wore his broad-brimmed hat and held the walking stick he never quite finished carving on.

"Dad?"

"Stay quiet, son. I need you to come with me."

"Am I in trouble?"

His father looked out across the creek beyond the campsite, like he might know something was out there waiting, and then back at his son. Tommy couldn't make out his father's expression under the canopy of oaks and American chestnuts.

What do you call nuts on your chest?

He could see the mustache against the shape of the man's face, but not much else. The thick mustache had long arms that came down on both sides of his mouth like a bandito mustache, or like a rogue cop on one of the late-night TV shows.

The silence and the pause felt dangerous.

"Why would you be in trouble?"

Because life is smudgy and you never can tell.

Tommy didn't know how to answer, so he stayed silent.

His father raised the end of his walking stick and Tommy flinched. "You missed some eyes. Retie your boots. We have a long way to go and I want to leave before anyone wakes up."

11

Tommy knelt and undid his laces in what little starlight stabbed through the leaves. "Where are we going?"

"Did I ask a question, or did I tell you what to do?"

Tommy dropped his head and pulled the laces tight to support his ankles for whatever was happening. He saw the foil blink at the edge of the fire circle where they had cooked beef, potatoes, and onions like hobos. Tommy hated onions at home, but rules of taste were suspended at campfires surrounded by darkness.

Tommy stood and his father led the way toward the creek. Tommy slipped twice negotiating the bank. Even with the shallow water over the rocks, the noise added deafness to blindness. Tommy had to tap with his foot to distinguish rock from water.

His father reached back with his free hand and Tommy leaned on the man's solid arm to keep his footing to the opposite bank. He felt his boots sticking to the tacky ground until they cleared the grasses and found themselves picking their way up the slope through the trees.

His father did not slow, but they were not following a clear-cut trail like they had in the previous day's hiking.

"Are you okay, son?"

The water was cold when I tried to pee. How did you know it was cold? I'm just blessed.

"I'm fine. Where are we going?"

"It's a long story."

They reached a ridge and followed along its spine. This marked the first time Tommy could remember his father having a long story that he wasn't telling, but which Tommy wanted to hear.

Sometimes, when his father thought the boys weren't listening, he'd tell the other men stories about the prison. He'd talk about how the prisoners weren't allowed to masturbate. If they were caught, they'd be punished by being hosed down outside, or forced to run laps naked in front of the other prisoners.

One of the assistant scout masters had said, "If I wasn't allowed to rub one out ever, I'd be as crazy as those polecats in the pokey, too."

The ridge failed and they weaved down into a series of washouts and pitted valleys. The tree cover separated above them. Starlight and a sliver of moon shone pale down into the gulches.

Tommy's father pulled him by his shoulder, sideways. With his father's hand staggering him, Tommy caught sight of a spit of bricks over broken boards and a dark pit.

"What's that?"

"An old well."

"I didn't know you could dig wells in mountains."

"Don't be a dummy."

"How deep does it go?"

"There's only one way to find out, isn't there?"

That's what your mom said.

Tommy began to realize "your mom" jokes didn't

work as well with family. His friends back home couldn't get enough of them.

They passed between the shells of cabins. The wheels and axles from a truck sank into the ground, covered in vines.

"What is this place?"

"A town that paid for what they did."

They passed a rusted bicycle frame that appeared to be swallowed by the trunk of a tree.

"You remember me telling you about your great, great uncle, Sully?"

Tommy stared at a broken wind chime dangling from a string of barbed wire. He started to speak, but then saw the word "Gomorrah" carved into the tree. He felt tempted to reach out and touch it to see if the bark was wet.

"Boy, am I talking to myself?"

"No, um, yes, I was told. Grandpa said one time he'd moved out to California before I was born, right?"

His father cleared his throat. Tommy realized he'd brought up grandpa. That sort of thing wasn't allowed in the real world. Maybe these haunted woods would protect him now though.

His father tapped the end of his walking stick on a stone. "Watch your shins. There's a fence up here, too."

Tommy stepped over the first stone and saw that it was a marker. He could not read the inscriptions through the mottled pattern of things that tended to grow only on forgotten tombstones. Tommy tried to jump aside, but he could not tell from the stones which way the bodies lay. He followed his father through the plots. His father tapped again and Tommy stepped carefully through the gap in the twisted, iron fence.

Tommy forced himself not to look back as they continued down the slope.

"Moving to California is code for someone in the family getting tied up in something people don't want known. In this part of the country, it can also mean … a man that likes … things that men in California like. We see that sort of debauchery in prison, too."

A man walks into a bar and offers twenty dollars to anyone that can cure his gas.

"Is that what happened to Uncle Sully?"

His father cleared his throat again. "Not by his choice."

Tommy made a face. This was another long story he did not want to hear.

Why did you let that guy do that to you? Because where I come from that's a bargain for twenty dollars.

Tommy saw a plow on its side against a stump as they passed a clearing.

"Great Uncle Sully was the second or third youngest of his brothers, and he was a science teacher. When your great grandfather was still in high school, Sully Rinder joined the Christian Education Initiative and came to teach up here in the mountains. The local town put him up in a room behind the chapel that served as the schoolhouse during the week. Churches along the

15

coast gave food and school supplies to the poor trash living in the mountains."

They walked over a blackened patch of ground. The dirt felt slimy under his boots. Tommy fought the temptation to feel if it was still warm.

His father continued, "Sully was not well received by the local boys that did not appreciate being made to learn all day and catch up on chores all evening. They made up stories about him to their parents, who were suspicious of Sully's performing science experiments in class. He got by okay for a while."

Tommy's father paused to poke at the ground. The skull and bones of a rodent lay arranged like a crucifix. The walking stick flipped the skull, showing sharp points at the snout. Tommy braced himself to be asked to identify the animal. It was too big to be a vole. It had the wrong shape for a squirrel.

His father walked on and Tommy followed.

"Sully had a way with the ladies and one of the young girls in town got sweet on him. They started seeing each other in secret. Some of the boys got wind of it and they told their parents, but Sully was slick and they could never catch him."

A girl asked the preacher, what's the difference between sin and shame? He answered that it is a sin to stick it in and a shame to take it out.

Tommy's father used his stick to move saplings aside. "They talked the girl into leading Sully out on the trail behind the chapel one night near Easter time.

He goes and suddenly catches a two-by-four across the teeth. She runs off and they beat Sully until his bones don't line up any longer. They tell him to crawl back to where he came from. Sully tells them to get in a line and screw each other. Instead, they drag him back to the schoolhouse, that also happens to be the chapel, and the story my father told me is … they take turns … taking him to California."

They passed a cinderblock foundation with charred lumber around the edges. Tommy stared at the blistered remains of the building and tried to ignore the bitter flavor of sleep still in his mouth.

"After they were done with him, they weren't done with him. They drug him out in front and strung him up on the Easter cross using barbed wire. They left him there, stripped, bleeding from the wrong places, and they still weren't done. They took the food the Christian Education Initiative sent and they smeared it all over him, and even up inside him. They thought the ants might find him and chew him up until he was discovered in the morning, and no teacher would ever use up their time again. It wasn't ants though. It was rats."

Tommy had heard his father tell the Ratman story before, but it was always a scientist that drank the wrong chemicals and changed, like Dr. Jekyll into Mr. Hyde. No one ever went to California in the other tellings.

She asked, "How long until the secret formula comes out?"

If you can still ask a question, you're not ready to drink it.

Tommy's father stepped into another clearing and stood in front of a cabin that looked more intact than the rest of the ghost town. Light began to paint the tops of the trees. Tommy could see rusty barbed wire strung along the eaves of the cabin like Christmas lights.

Tommy whispered, "What is this?"

If she has to ask, you're doing something wrong.

"The rats didn't just bite him. They hollowed him out and filled him up. The next morning, they didn't find him strung up. They didn't find anything. Then they started finding the bones of the boys laid out like a crucifix. Some tried to flee deeper into the mountains, but the king rat, the Ratman, followed."

"What's wrong with you?" Tommy said. "Why would you wake me up to play a prank like this?"

His father grabbed his ear and pulled him forward. "Boy, since before you were born, men have been coming up here once a week to feed a legend, and your grandpa before me never stopped trying to find his soul, still somewhere in the writhing mass under his skin. Trying to keep the monster that curses this family from hunting farther away from these ruins. The prank is being born a Rinder."

When his father mentioned grandpa for the first time in as long as Tommy could remember, the boy's fear doubled upon itself.

"Dad, stop." The side of Tommy's head started to get hot with pain and irritation, but Dad wouldn't let go.

"Once I had the responsibility dumped on me, along with work and family and everything else, I couldn't get up here as often as my superstitious father could," Dad said. "Bad things started happening, so I tried to start coming again, but couldn't never find Sully up here myself to confirm things. He wouldn't meet me like he supposedly did my father before me, my grandfather before him, or his own nephews in between all that."

"Dad, you're hurting me. Please, I didn't do anything this time."

"Now that the killing has started again, I think it's too late."

Carter Rinder tapped the head of his stick against the door twice and then kicked it open. Tommy tried to pull back, hard enough to tear his own ear off, but his father pulled him inside by the nape of his neck.

3

Sheets covered the windows and a mattress rotted on a cot in the corner. Bones dangled from hooks on wires strung across the ceiling. A shirt hung in the middle of the room, nearer the back wall.

Tommy's father reached out and yanked the tan shirt down. He held it up and cursed.

"This belongs to you. This is your extra. He's been to the camp. Let's go."

His father ran out the door with the shirt. Tommy followed and raced after his father.

"This isn't funny, Dad."

His father would not slow. His hat fell off, but he did not stop. Tommy grabbed it up and kept running.

His father's foot broke through the boards and he collapsed over the well. Tommy grabbed his father's shoulders and pulled. The man's leg came out bloody. Tommy cursed worse than he had in the tent. His father

20

pushed him aside and staggered forward on his bloody leg.

I'm sore. Tell your mother to stop using her teeth so much.

His father was halfway across the creek by the time Tommy caught up. He didn't bother using the stepping stones. His father stared at a tree when Tommy walked up beside him, panting.

His father pointed. Tommy saw in the weak light of morning the words "Leave now" carved in the bark.

His father handed Tommy back his shirt and said, "Don't tell anyone about this. I'm going to tend my leg and then we'll get everyone out of here while we still can. Wipe that off before they wake up. He's angry that I brought all these boys. He hates boys."

His father limped away. Tommy couldn't tell if his father was smiling at his sick joke, or if he was sneering in pain.

You'd limp, too, if you carried this much weight between your legs.

Tommy stepped closer and realized the words weren't carved, but written in ash.

He looked over after his father, crawling back into his tent on his injury, and wondered if his dad would suffer through a bloody leg for a prank. He looked up at the words in ash and then down at his extra shirt that his dad had left in the boy's hands. And maybe had posed in a cabin dressed up like a grindhouse horror movie. He wondered what kind of thinking and feeling was behind a prank like that, or what mind could create the story to go with it. It was almost more disturbing for Tommy to imagine it all as a father's prank than a true story. His sleep-deprived, adrenaline-flooded brain wouldn't settle on either option as the truth.

Ratman

The word was going to stick with him and crawl around inside him. He could feel that was true.

Tommy reached up with his extra uniform shirt and rubbed away the smudged letters. He wanted to leave more than anything, whether the story was true or not.

Tommy Rinder was watched from across the creek.

Promises were made, promises were broken, and it was too late to make things right again.

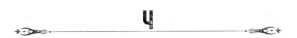

They broke promises and they mocked their own betrayal.

He watched them with his hollow eyes and thought about killing them right then. They deserved it. It needed to happen. He did not move from the brush beside the creek, though. Not right away.

He could not remember exactly who he was, back when he was Sully Rinder. He tried. Sometimes he almost remembered the girl, the one he thought he had loved back when he lived. Then, he'd remember the torture. He'd remember the rats. He'd remember the family who'd promise to come make it right after he killed and fed on every last person in Gomorrah.

From the brush across the water, his empty eyes watched the Rinders and the other boys and men packing their vehicles. He watched them drive away.

As he stood there alone for hours, still watching, his

sockets weren't ever truly empty. Fur brushed by the stretched openings, nearly catching the light. Beady black eyes, deeper in his head, would glint a moment and then be gone. A tough pink tail would flick by or poke out like an alien tentacle, but then retreat back into the dark, hot safety of his head.

Then, he realized why he had not killed them then and there.

Because there were more Rinders. More of them, from the last generations of the family, back where he used to call home. The family broke the promise, so the family needed to end. All of them needed to pay.

The sun traveled the sky long after they had left. He knew what he needed to do now. He knew where he needed to go.

But he needed to feed. He needed to grow.

It was time.

He stepped out of the brush and stood at the water's edge. If anyone were there to see this sight in the afternoon sun, they would have likely died of fright on the spot. If they survived, they'd have seen the shape of the man with his skin stretched to nearly seven feet tall. The skin moved and changed shape as things inside shifted around. The eyes appeared to be empty black holes. The mouth was toothless and, whenever the lips were stretched open by movement inside the body, small beady eyes stared out from the darkness within by the dozens.

The lips started to move on their own, and a voice that

sounded like wind through a graveyard fence issued a single word from the mouth that used to belong to Sully, "Feed."

The movement within the flesh of the seven foot tall body turned frantic. Rats poured out of the skin from the mouth and ears, and other holes in the stretched flesh. The rodents crawled over the top of each other along the creek bank.

As they emptied out of the body, the skin deflated until it lay as a discarded pile in the mud. Some of the rats attacked each other now that they were free of the body that contained them and controlled them.

They had a mission, though, so they spread out through the field and into the woods, attacking other living things, consuming them, growing.

They found other rats: brown, grey, and black. Sometimes they attacked. Sometimes the rodents spoke with a windy voice that was not their own, "Return to me."

The new rats followed the old and, one after another, they crawled back into the skin beside the bank. They packed in together as the body started to fill. The skin stretched as the rats returned to fill and serve their king. Once they were all back, the man of rats stood ten feet tall in his stretched and strained skin.

He stretched his arms, rolled his back, and flexed his fingers. Using the rats as his muscles, he bent his legs and took a step. Using the minds of the rats as his own, the Ratman knew where he needed to go and how to get there. With their breath and their furry bodies as his tongue, he said, "Rinder."

Ratman crossed the river in two strides on his now-longer legs. Fingers full of rat tails for bone and muscle gripped the bank and the trees as he pulled himself up.

Using their pink noses, he sniffed the smell of the old fire and the stink their bodies left behind. He smelled the lingering exhaust from their engines, and he followed their trail out of the abandoned campsite and along the path as darkness settled through the woods.

The game warden's light came on from off the trail to the left. It passed over the shadowy figure walking through the forest long after the last of the sunlight died. A guy wandering out here at night, where the last registered campers had left, was probably up to no good.

The game warden's name was Alan Hooker. He was a decent fellow, who loved wildlife. His hero was Teddy Roosevelt, who started the National Park System, and he believed in conservation and responsible hunting. He was still a fan of Richard Nixon, even after Watergate, because of the environmental legislation he'd passed.

Alan's wife had left him and taken the kids, partly because of drinking, and partly for too many other reasons to name. He'd never hit her, although he'd thought about it toward the end.

He'd just started dating a girl in the sheriff's department in the county where he lived. An honest-to-God girl deputy, who filled out her uniform nicely.

Unlike his ex, she understood having to work long hours. He'd met her while collaborating with the local law on some poachers who were also growing pot in the backwoods of the parks.

Those guys had up and vanished, but Alan was out, seeing if he could hunt them up tonight. And here this tall drink of water was just strolling along, out where no one was registered to be.

If Alan was honest, he was out here partly to catch them, and partly to impress Stephanie. "Game warden. Stop there just a moment."

The Ratman saw the light and heard the voice, but it came from no one who concerned him or the broken promises. He smelled a few broken promises on the man, but they were old ones, and it wasn't enough to spark the monster's fury. If he hadn't just fed, Alan would have been in more trouble, but the hundreds of bellies inside him were mostly full. So, he walked on and the game warden had a chance to live.

Warden Hooker stepped out in the road behind the walking figure and demanded, "I told you to stop. I'll stop you, myself, if you make me. Just stop and talk to me. Hands where I can see them."

Ratman kept walking, though dozens of ears perked up within him and his rat muscles shifted uneasily.

Alan ran forward. His flashlight bobbed as he caught up and he rested his hand on his holstered weapon.

The rats opened their jaws and bared their teeth inside the body. Their king hadn't given the order yet.

28

They would not act until he did. But they knew it was coming.

Alan knew something was wrong when he grabbed the arm, that was both cold and hot in spots, and felt the movement under the flesh. His next thought was *Big Foot,* when he got a better feel for the scale of this man.

"Release," the inhuman voice hissed with rats' breath.

The rodents poured out of their king and fell upon Alan Hooker, en masse. He screamed, but the rats filled his mouth and chewed his cheeks from the inside. The newer rat recruits wanted to impress their king. They tore Alan's uniform and squirmed inside before chewing their way into the flesh between his ribs. Skin peeled away from muscle, and muscle from bone, before Alan finally expired. His last thought in this world was realizing that they were attacking his eyes.

The Ratman was almost eleven feet tall when he started walking again.

5

Tommy Rinder had to unload the station wagon himself when they got home to Butler, South Carolina late that afternoon, to their house on Jeff Davis Road, across from the cow pasture. Dad was inside with Mom, Tamatha Hucks Rinder, who went by Tammy and was helping tend to Carter's leg.

Alan Hooker was driving up to his last stakeout in the park, listening to "Everybody Plays the Fool" by The Main Ingredient on the radio, at the moment Carter Rinder yelled at his wife, loud enough for Tommy to hear outside, "I can't go to the doctor. It's Sunday and I can't miss work tomorrow."

"When gangrene sets in and you get it cut off," she said, "then you'll be a one-legged guard."

Carter balled his fists. "I'm not in the mood to listen to a …"

She looked up from the scrapes on his legs and met

his eyes. She wasn't a big woman, but she wasn't slight, either. If it came to it, she would lose badly in a fight, but she might also get ahold of something and open his skull, if he ever tried. The theory had never been tested.

Her second cousin was the county sheriff. They weren't close, but if a Rinder got brought in for domestic on a woman with Hucks as a maiden name, that wouldn't go over well. The fact that the sheriff's daddy was a judge wouldn't help things either.

Carter wasn't the kind of man who needed these reasons not to lay a hand on his wife, but they were fine reminders, just the same, when he was tired, hurt, or had a shift involving urine thrown in his face by some rapist or drug addict sodomite in D Block.

"What?" she asked flatly. "Some what?"

"Some woman who is well-kept by a man who doesn't miss work for cuts and scrapes, and should be grateful for it."

"Eternally grateful, love." She applied a hearty helping of rubbing alcohol on the next cotton swab before she drew it across the nastier of the cuts.

He hissed and gripped the arms of the chair, but didn't comment. He knew why she did it, and she knew he was going to give it back to her rough in a different sort of way, after the kids went to bed.

He smiled at her and smoothed down his mustache with the forefinger and thumb of one hand. She smiled back.

* * *

It would be almost a week later when two sheriff's deputies would come upon the bones, several yards off the trails back in the park, near the campground's let-out. It was still daylight at the time of the discovery, but it came filtered through the thick greenery above, so they still used their flashlights.

Some of the bones were tied off with sections of barbed wire, dangling from the branches in a haphazard pattern that could almost pass for art.

The larger bones lay on the ground, under this display. The bones on the ground formed the shape of a cross that was upside down from the perspective of where the deputies stood.

The skull, clearly human, sat on its teeth, staring hollow-eyed away from the other bones and at the deputies' boots in the clover, in this secluded pocket of growth. The bottom jawbone of the victim twirled at eye-level from a piece of rusty barbed wire.

"After the sheriff, we're going to have to call in state on this horror-house scene," Deputy Stine said.

Deputy Faust was younger than Stein, newer on the job. He misheard Stine as saying, "whore house scene." He spent another couple seconds trying to figure out what bones spread around like this had to do with whorehouses, but came up empty. He didn't want to sound stupid, so Faust just said, "Yeah, I guess so."

Neither of them was a forensic expert. Wasn't much

of that in this part of the hills, at this point in time anyway, but bones devoid of meat and laying out like this, disconnected from one another, would lead them to think this was an old scene. The flies and bits of gristle still attached to a few of the bigger bones messed with that calculation a little.

Stein knelt down and poked at a few of the bones with his bare finger. Faust thought that might not be a good idea, but maybe it didn't matter. Finding prints out in the open like this was a long-shot anyway.

Stein was focused on the narrow scratches over all the bones. He pictured a knife pulling the meat off, like a hunter cleaning a kill. He'd have never come around to figuring out it was rats' teeth that made those marks.

He did uncover a wallet and picked it up to find everything inside. Before he looked at the I.D., he thought how colossally stupid criminals were. He was sure he could get away with crimes way better than people who actually committed them.

Stein paused over the license and the game warden I.D. he found. Game wardens were the least favorite law enforcement in the area. They could ruin a man's life if he hunted over the wrong invisible line, baited the ducks with too much corn, or forgot to renew. They could saunter over any jurisdiction, and enforce any law, from federal on down. Most of the deputies were hunters and didn't care for the wardens much. When the girl came on the force, that was bad enough, but when she started dating a game warden …

Stein said, "Tell me the name of that fella who stood up Stephanie Greer."

Faust thought about it. "Alex or Alvin. Something like that. I only met him on that joint investigation that went nowhere."

"His last name?" Deputy Stein said.

That was easy. It was like the old general, or the word for prostitutes. "Hooker, wasn't it?"

Stein pictured angry hunters, maybe those same drug pushers they'd been tailing up here a couple weeks ago, scraping the meat from Hooker's bones with their buck knives. Maybe they were Satanist cultists, too. Cannibals, to boot. Some real Charles Manson stuff going on, right here in their backyard.

He closed the wallet and pocketed it as he stood. "We'll need to let the sheriff break it to Deputy Greer what we found up here. Probably going to have to get the FBI involved."

By the time they'd found Alan Hooker's bones, the destruction in Butler, South Carolina, down in Rutledge County, was long over.

Jay Wilburn

6

About the same time Tommy Rinder hopped on his bike to go meet his friends at the scrapyard on Monday morning, all four members of the Collier family died in a bad way going southbound on Braxton Bragg Highway, a few miles north of the state line between North and South Carolina. That's not to be confused with Braxton Bragg Lane, Avenue, Court, or the three streets called Braxton Bragg Road scattered across the South. Getting them confused would be understandable, as in the last year of the 1970s all seven of those roads were two lane and cut through the middle of nowhere.

The highway had acres of farmland behind barbed wire on the right, as you went south, and pine forest on the left. It wasn't the main route going through the Carolinas at the time, which is why a monster made of human skin and full of rats, now seventeen feet tall, could walk through the night and into the morning unnoticed.

Paul Collier sold timeshares from offices in Virginia Beach, the Outer Banks, Myrtle Beach, and Savannah, which accounted for one hundred percent of their family's working vacations, much to Darla's silent disappointment. Seven-year-old Collin and five-year-old Skylar didn't know the difference.

He prided himself on finding the most creative shortcuts, the least traffic, and best driving times. He loved to save and catch a discount more than the experiences attached. Darla was silent on this, too.

That's why they were the lone car on Braxton Brigg Highway, in the rising heat of that July Monday morning, and why Paul got his whole family killed.

He saw the Ratman first. The figure was tall and misshapen, like the thing had been covered in rubber and then allowed to age there in the sun for years. It looked naked and Paul got a little ticked that the local government of whatever town covered these boonies would allow this to continue.

For a moment, he swore it was moving, lumbering along the wide, grassy shoulder between the highway and the fence line, and Paul's blood went cold enough that he almost shivered. He almost swerved away from it. He almost laid down on the accelerator and gave up all his good gas mileage.

He raced past it with his heart thudding in his chest, as he took deep breaths to steady himself behind the wheel. He wouldn't look in the rearview. He didn't have any desire to see what sort of rubbery face the rednecks who erected that thing had put on their abomination.

Darla saw it, too, but stayed silent, kind of hoping the kids didn't notice. She wished, not for the last time that day, that they had taken a major highway instead.

The kids noticed.

"That statue's moving," Collin said.

"I'm scared," Skylar screamed, in that tone where it was impossible to tell if she was really afraid or seeking attention. Paul thought the girl screamed every word she'd ever said since she learned to talk. She was the exact opposite of her mother.

In less than a minute, Skylar would scream the rest of her life, and it would be the last thing they all heard.

"Stop it, Collin," Paul said, "you're scaring your sister."

He was scaring his father, too.

Something slid in the floorboard around Paul's feet, giving him chills. He really did shiver then. He thought it was one of the kids' loose toys. Such a thing could get under the brake and kill them all.

He was about to yell at the kids about that, but then Darla started screaming. It didn't last long, but it was like all the screams she had stored up over the years coming out at once. It was enough for Paul to swerve into the wrong lane of the empty road and then overcompensate on the way back.

A half dozen rats, as black as shadows, latched onto Darla. She went pale and silent as Skylar started screaming and Collin made a guttural choking noise.

The rats climbed up Paul's pant legs and tore into his clothes from all sides.

The car left the road and raked along the barbwire on the passenger's side, shattering the headlight on the posts.

Paul didn't have long left to think, but in that time of panic, he did manage to regret never taking Darla to the Caribbean or to California like he'd promised when he got into this business. He thought about how he'd dreamed of his kids going to college without having to work their way through, like he did.

Darla thought about the kids. Even as she bled out, she climbed over the seat to fight the rodents in the back instead of the ones killing her. She wished they were on a main highway, where help would come sooner.

She pulled three rats, by their tails, out of her son's mouth, but couldn't get the rest before they climbed in his bulging throat and choked him as they chewed. The ones she pulled out turned on her and bathed in her blood as they attacked.

Before she lost her eyes to them, she swatted other rats away from her daughter hard enough to bounce them off the inside of the door. They took ragged strips of flesh with them, and fought each other for the pieces.

The last things she saw were her son's blackened face and her children's bones showing through their deepest wounds. The last she heard was her daughter's unending screams.

The Ratman watched the car finally come to a stop, far ahead in the distance. As his rat servants emptied out of him, he came to rest on the side of the highway. He didn't know how long he remained like that, but as they filled him again, he returned to his full height and covered the distance between himself and the car that was tangled up in the fence.

In life, the man who had been Sully Rinder enjoyed walking barefoot in the grass as the Ratman did now. The Ratman really didn't feel the grass through the skin of his feet filled full of waiting rats, flexing their bodies in place of his muscles with each step.

More rodents answered the call. Field mice joined the country rats as they ran through the grass, climbed the giant's body, and crawled in with the rats. Inside, the rats made to attack the mice. The motion warped the Ratman's flesh for a moment but, eventually, the survivors settled into the roles they served within him.

By the time he reached the car, he stood twenty-three feet tall and couldn't get his fingers, now full of rats and not just their tails, inside the vehicle. In frustration, he tore off the doors and the roof of the car, to the sound of shattering glass. The last few rats that were left picking the bones clean climbed up the arms of their king and shifted around inside.

As he fumbled the delicate bones, he waited a moment. The rats shifted around inside him at their king's wishes. His stretched flesh appeared to roil about in a wild, frenzied motion. The field mice climbed down between the packed bodies of the rats and they finally filled in his fingers, giving him the fine-motor control he needed.

As he gathered the pieces, the Ratman pulled the barbed wire away from the side of the car and from the posts. The barbs cut his palms and pierced the bodies of the rats inside. They remained still and obedient, even as they bled.

Ratman crossed the road, standing nearly as tall as the pines, and began stringing up the pieces. He even hung up the car doors and the roof, causing the trees to bow.

As he worked, squirrels jumped between the branches to escape. Then, they changed their small minds. They understood their purpose finally. As the squirrels crawled into the Ratman, another conflict erupted. Ratman allowed it to play out as he finished his work.

By the time he finished the bone crosses on the centerline of Braxton Bragg Highway, he stood twenty-six feet tall. He returned to the grass and continued south.

The crosses were made of a combination of bones from four different skeletons.

The next traveler to pass wasn't until hours later, in the early evening. John Stein, a distant cousin twice removed from Deputy Stein farther north, who wouldn't discover Game Warden Hooker's body for almost a week, crept down the center of the highway high upon his tractor. He missed the pieces of car and bone strung up in the shadows of the pines because he was staring at the wreckage of the car on the other side.

The thing was stripped down enough to where it looked old. A wide swatch of fence was down in the same area. John pondered this as he drove straddle over the bone crosses without seeing them. His front wheels crushed a pelvis bone and a small skull, but he didn't hear it over the engine.

Buzzards returned to the bones after the tractor passed.

A fat grey rat, who had been left behind by his king, ran into the road and caught hold of a piece of metal hanging low behind the tractor. Its lonely and lost eyes glowed red as it climbed up behind John to feed for its king.

A small voice, not its own, whispered, "Give him your bones."

Then the glow went out of the creature's gaze. It woke up from its long trance and looked around in confusion. Finally, the rat jumped off to a heavy landing in the dark street. It wandered into the grass to return to a normal life of foraging.

By this point, the Ratman was deep into South Carolina and still growing, still walking.

Tommy's dad was in a foul mood, even for him, even for a Monday. It could have been having to go back to work after driving home from the campout the day before. The man had said himself how bad he was going to feel, even before they'd left, right after he got off work on Friday. Tommy didn't consider that it was Carter Rinder's foot festering inside his work boot that accounted for the extra darkness in the man that morning.

Tommy had forgotten about his father's foot, but not the strange trip and strange story for an even stranger prank. He'd failed to ask his father why he'd done it before they left the woods. Now that they were back in the real world, the smudgy rules of camping were over. There was no asking questions like that, now, without repercussions.

44

But that story …

Ratman.

His friends were out and playing early. Dad left for the prison early, but not exactly with the sun that started a day of summer play. Tommy had never been told to directly, but he always waited until his father left before he ran out to play. He had an intuition that his father resented kids playing, with no responsibility, when he had to work all day surrounded by dangerous lowlifes.

The Ratman … he doesn't like boys …

Carter Rinder drove south on Jeff Davis, finally, after taking longer than usual to get up from his coffee and paper. Tommy sprinted for his bike, with his sisters following close behind.

They were a pair of devils, in Tommy's eyes, those two. Carter had taken Tommy to see *The Frisco Kid* in the movie theater the weekend before the campout. There had been a teaser trailer for a scary movie called *The Shining*, coming out the next summer. The trailer had ended with a boy on a big wheel, staring at a pair of twin girls at the end of a hallway, with a music cue that made Tommy jump. Carter had laughed at the scene, or at Tommy, or both. His sisters weren't twins, and didn't usually dress alike, but he thought of Ashley and Holly Anne after that jump scare.

Ashley, two years younger than Tommy, was only an inch taller than Holly Anne, two years younger than her. Both wore jeans with floweredy patterns in the

45

stitching. Holly Anne was still dressed by Mom and wore shirts with puffy sleeves, and butterfly barrettes to hold up long blond pigtails. Ashley dressed herself in oversized t-shirts with elastic at the ends of the short sleeves, and her browner hair hung down straight over her ears and eyes.

"You need to stay and help us," Holly Anne said.

"There's no help for you." Tommy walked out to the end of the driveway before mounting up on his bike.

"Dad said you knew how to rehang the swing," Holly Anne insisted.

"I'll do it when I get home," Tommy said.

"He's just in a bad mood because Dad made him get a haircut," Ashley said. "Now he can't look like David Cassidy."

That stung a little. He did want his hair longer, but that was a "no go" with Dad. It wasn't some stupid singer though. He wanted to be Ponch, but to look like John from CHiPs.

Tommy kicked off and headed north on Jeff Davis, the opposite direction as his father.

"We're telling Dad you didn't help when he gets home," Holly Anne yelled shrilly at his back. "You better get home and help us before he does, or you'll get it."

Sweat already broke out along his hairline and under his shirt. It was going to be hot as hell with humidity. He fought against the slight incline of the road going this way, that he only ever noticed on his bike.

"Go help yourself into a sewer pipe." He didn't say it loud enough for them to hear, but it still felt like a good burn.

He beat the incline and picked up speed, trying to get to the scrapyard before he missed everything. The place was owned by Mace Finch, who was a bit of a crime legend around town. Kids told stories of gunfights between the Finches and their rivals that couldn't be true in the real world. It added to the inherent dangers and mysteries of jagged metal and apocalyptic junk that stretched back from the road for miles.

Scrapyards, even ones this epic, were too low a place for someone like Mace Finch to stand guard. He owned other places, where men shot pool and played poker in back rooms. Mace hired an idiot old man everyone called Mr. Lips to guard it. Kids weren't kind when describing people by their looks. Mr. Lips was called worse on the rare occasions he made an effort to chase kids out of the vast maze of dirt paths around and between junk cars and other piles of appliances and trash. The low-paid guard was slow, mentally and physically, but still the kind you pedaled hard to escape from, if he took a mind to chase.

On a day like today, Mr. Lips was going to stay in the shack at the gate, letting people in and checking them out for cash. No one would be looking for alternators or the guts of an old refrigerator on a blazing day like today. Mr. Lips would be drinking and dozing in the sweltering shade of the shack by the road.

Tommy left the road and followed the southern edge of the chain link that barely contained the place. The dirt track was rutted and awful, but it was familiar ground for Tommy. He passed the first two openings in the fence before cutting into the third break in the fence line.

The stacks of cars waiting to be crushed or hauled away were piled six high on both sides, and the path between them grew quite narrow as Tommy rode his bike deeper into the wondrous scrapyard.

He started to suspect where his friends were. He knew the area they claimed as theirs, but he hated that dark place, where it felt like the floor was going to fall through under you at any moment, to God-knew-what underneath.

As he drew closer, the cars were stacked eight and ten high, in wavering lines, where the piles tipped and leaned against each other. That couldn't be safe. Maybe not even legal, and Tommy suspected they were going to get crushed and never found again out here. They'd be some of those missing kids folks put on milk cartons, or on posters about runaways up on all the poles along the beach.

They were here, he knew. They had gone where Tommy feared. In a strange little pocket of debris deep in the yard, where the junked cars all leaned into the center like being drawn into a vortex, a wooden house stood penned in, with the broken roof hidden behind fields of metal.

Tommy never could figure out why this house was here, or what it had once been. Three bedrooms and two bathrooms, although every appliance and bit of plumbing had been torn out except for the most stubborn pipes sticking out of leaning and spongy walls that never dried out, even in prolonged heat like this.

He pushed his bike through the narrow pass, with sharp thorns of rusted metal reaching out to cut him and infect him with tetanus or lockjaw, that mothers terrified their wild boys with to get them to wear shoes on their all-day adventures. It worked on Tommy. He loved the scrapyard like a brave knight loves the kingdom he defends from monsters, but he felt the danger around him like an electricity traveling the air and passing through him. He felt it the most when rolling his bike into the shadows of "The House".

The boards threatened under every step he took. Dirty light twisted in between cars and through the scant glass they hadn't yet broken with rocks. They hadn't left much. Tommy was surprised there was any, after all their time here. He suspected the dirty glass grew back at night. He knew that wasn't possible, same as he knew light didn't bend to find its way through broken windows of abandoned houses but, like the woods and like the surface of the jagged glass, things were smudgy here. Parents' rules still held sometimes, but only loosely, like from across a portal into another dimension.

How tight do you want me to hold it? Until it screams for

you to stop and not a moment sooner!

If his mother saw this place, or half the things they did here, she would die and call Tommy's father to whip the devil out of him. They were different people here. They were some other species of creature, almost like the boys they were outside the scrapyard, in a similar shape as the human kids who still said, "Yes, sir," and helped set tables for dinner.

He found himself thinking about his shirt hanging up in that old cabin at the end of his father's bizarre story, and he shivered in the stuffy heat of The House.

The stack of dirty magazines, with water stains on the covers and pages, were stacked in the corner of a closet, leaning like the junk cars pressing against The House.

The other boys weren't here.

The kitchen, with the thin pipe coming out where the stove used to be, was empty, too. There was a flexible metal hose clamped onto the pipe and holes broken in the floor around it. Oven mitts sat on top of the pipe for an experiment they were never likely going to get to work, and Tommy hoped never would work.

He walked his bike out the open back of The House and rolled through another box canyon of sharp metal.

Here they were.

Bobby King and Shawn Spitz, both thirteen like Tommy, leaned against a hood with no car to go with it, propped against a gutted industrial freezer on its side. From there, they threw screws and broken bolt heads at a dead rat the size of a cat.

Bobby was fatter than Tommy, while Spitz was thinner. Bobby was tallest, and Spitz shortest. Bobby's hair blond and military short. Spitz's hair was dark and hung long all around and curled up at the ends like a Duke Boy. Tommy wanted his hair like that, but not as greasy.

Tommy dropped his bike on top of the other two and they scooted over for him on the hood. Spitz handed some of his screws and bolts to Tommy. Bobby thumped the dead rat's bloated belly with a bolt, to the sound of flicking a ripe melon. The patchy flesh split and clear liquid seeped out like watered-down Cairo syrup. Tommy thought he could see the stink and disease rising off the carcass in wavering lines of heat, like in the cartoons.

Tommy missed the rat on purpose with his throws. "Did you guys kill it yourselves?"

"Nah," Bobby said, from the other side of Spitz, "it got into some of Mr. Lips' poison somewhere. They smell different when they've been poisoned."

Tommy's stomach turned as he registered the ripe smell of death in high July heat in the low country of South Carolina. Some days it was ten degrees cooler at the beach, a drop in degree for each mile, but he suspected today was a day where he wouldn't find cooler temperatures unless he kept going and swam to the bottom of the ocean.

"You need to toss lower or throw softer," Spitz said.

"You keep overshooting it."

"Yeah, I'll get the hang of it," Tommy said.

Bobby asked, "What did the sign on the outside of the whorehouse say?"

Spitz said, "Beat it. We're closed."

"No," Bobby said. "Your mother's busy. Come back later."

Spitz said, "What's the difference between a tire and 365 rubbers?"

"Your mom doesn't need new tires," Bobby said.

Spitz rolled his eyes. "One's a Goodyear. The other's a great year."

Jokes that only work on campouts and in the scrapyard,
Tommy thought

They left the rat and explored the yard, finding nothing new, but inventing new worlds of apocalyptic glory worthy of a sci fi story from a Heavy Metal mag. Instead of dragons, Tommy pictured ratmen and his play took on a harder edge that day.

The crushers weren't running today. The boys looked around for Mr. Lips, or any adults who might be there for legitimate business. Then, they climbed up onto the platform above the control station. They peered over the sides into the metal pit. The walls looked scratched and scarred, like the last metal dropped inside had tried to claw its way back out and failed.

Tommy imagined some grand alien robot being crushed to death.

Voices echoed from some distance and the boys

climbed back down in a hurry. They returned to playing farther away from these machines.

By eleven o'clock, Tommy was ready to bail for Kool-Aide and lunch. They could show up at any of their houses, but Spitz was closest. His mother would make them grilled cheese with two slices and any soup they wanted.

Bobby was the farthest, closer to the beach, a couple miles from a fleabag motel his parents ran. They usually didn't go out there.

"I got quarters," Bobby said. "Let's go to the beach."

Quarters could mean the arcade, it could mean comic books, it could mean ice cream, but it also meant a ten-mile bike ride farther than his mother ever wanted Tommy to go.

The problem was, his friends were already suspicious of him missing the rat with every throw, so Tommy went along after Spitz said okay.

Besides, Bobby had quarters.

8

About the time Guard Carter Rinder was getting bad news at the prison, Ratman killed 32 snowbirds and the driver of their bus on Highway 52, somewhere between Coward and Lake City.

Roxie Stanton was already ticked off. She sat at the front of the bus with her arms crossed over her ample, but sagging, bosom. The old girls had stood up well into her sixties, but when they started to go, they went fast. Now, her flesh sagged to the point she could almost tuck her breasts into her pants. The filling had gone right out of the pillows.

Lots of things bothered Roxie. Joseph hadn't left her with enough to keep their house. After her hip went, she had to go into assisted care, and these group trips were as extravagant as she could get. They were already getting to Charleston late and going to miss a whole day. They'd probably have a fast food dinner, too.

All that bothered her, but Agnes, in the back of the bus, bothered her the most. Everyone had chosen sides. The laughter in the back half of the bus felt so fake and so insulting. Roxie's friends, fewer in number, were sullen in the front, also upset about how things were going.

It wasn't just that Agnes made the plans for the whole group. She had promised things that weren't delivered. Roxie never expected her to, but it was the principle of the thing. It was that she purposely decided for everyone that ...

Windows shattered out of Roxie's side of the bus and the whole vehicle rippled in two directions as the structure bent from the impact. The driver tried to compensate, to counter the sickening feel of the tilting weight on two wheels.

Roxie forgot all about Agnes as the windshield, as big as a plate glass window, exploded inward and outward at the same time. She only caught a glimpse as the driver was snatched right from his seat by the hand of a god.

The unattended steering wheel rolled with lazy momentum as the bus careened off the road. The wheels bounded through ruts in the grass, sending elderly women from their seats hard enough to shatter bones.

Their bones were so brittle that, by the time the rats stripped them clean, Ratman had to use a number of splinters to make his crosses later.

Hatches sprung open along the bottom of the bus and spilled luggage blasted its contents across the access road, exposing the ladies' delicates. Some of the old birds had snuck their hard shell suitcases into the bus because they did not trust the driver. Five women were concussed bloody by the loose luggage inside. Agnes shattered three bones in her face from one of the cases, and swallowed her dentures, beginning to choke to death.

The bus crashed through a liquor store called Confederate Package and Rebel Spirits. The clerk looked up a moment before the counter splintered and he was taken under the wheels. It took him a long time to die in the pool of mixed liquor that filled the floor in waves, from countless shattered bottles, after the bus barreled out from the demolished storerooms.

Ratman followed the bus at a casual pace, but being fifty feet tall now, the monster kept up easily.

The driver screamed as he felt the rat bodies through the skin of the giant's hand gripping him. He had no idea what that sensation was until the Ratman stuffed the driver through his rubbery lips. His terror was around the idea of being eaten alive. He waited for the feel of giant teeth slicing through his body like multiple guillotines.

When the rats covered him over and pierced him with hundreds of tiny teeth, he forgot all about the giant. He screamed, even as the rats took his open mouth as an invitation. They writhed over the top of him inside their king's skin. The motion pulled him down deeper into the Ratman's body. More rats fought each other in order to get close enough.

The driver continued to scream long after most of his flesh was ripped from his bones. Until the rats burrowed in deep enough to eat his lungs, too, he screamed.

The Ratman's flesh twisted and bubbled with the war going on inside. The screams carried up and out the opening of his stretched lips, as his hollow eyes tracked the careening bus. Since the screams left his mouth, the Ratman thought they were his screams, but he didn't know why he was screaming. Hunger? Anger? Rage at the broken promises? It didn't matter much. He would feed, and he would collect their bones.

The bus made a gradual turn as it crossed a gravel lot and then tore the front of a department store called Dixie's Dandies off the building. Bargain bins obliterated. Cash registers in the closed store tore away and dinged open before coming apart. A riding lawnmower on display in the front folded under the weight of the bus, but ramped it up and finally tipped the vehicle over.

There was no driver to save them this time. The rats inside the giant had just torn into the sacs of the driver's lungs, within his stripped skeleton. Roxie tumbled between the seats as the bus slid to a stop on its side, and a few bodies landed on top of her, separating a rib and forcing the air out of her.

57

Agnes bounced around and took some hard shots she would not recover from, but she was still trying to cough up a denture plate.

Ratman punched through the accordion door to the bus, but couldn't fit his arm in far enough to grab any of the screaming women. He reached through the windshield, but many of the ones he could reach were jammed between the seats.

The giant lowered to his soft knees in the gravel. "Feed … Bring me … their bones."

He emptied out as the rodents poured through the broken windows and the real screaming began. The rats brought out a few, but not all, of the driver's bones from within their king. They left the offering beside the pile of skin as they scoured the bus to clean and collect more bones.

Of the 33 women from the Sunny Vale Assisted Living Facility on the Charleston trip that year, only one, Roxie Stanton, survived the day. She passed out from lack of oxygen, and would have suffocated, except that the rats fed and removed all the weight piled on top of her.

They would have kept feeding until they got down to her, but the Ratman's call to return with an offering of bones was too great for them to resist. With their bellies swollen and ready to burst, the rodents brought out bones and pieces of bones from the skeletons after the thin and aged flesh was no more.

As her starved brain caught up on oxygen, she heard the rats say, "Bring him the bones."

The rats piled the bones in front of the bus and refilled the skin. As the Ratman stood back to his full height, towering over the scene, he noticed the one trying to get away, leaving a trail of blood in the gravel. He almost let her go, but then he got a sense. It was something only he was sensitive enough to feel. She had broken a promise recently, to a lot of people, so he pursued her.

Agnes had been on the verge of death, from the plastic wedged tight in her throat, as the rats reached her in the back of the bus last. They tore her paper-thin skin and she bled. One of the rats ripped a hole in her throat below the obstruction and she sucked in air in a wet rush of relief.

Before Agnes was aware of the horrors going on around her, the rats disengaged and started collecting bones for their king. She might have survived like Roxie, except that she fumbled around herself for something to grab and opened the emergency door, tumbling backward onto the gravel.

It took Agnes a while to climb to her feet with her wounds and fractures. She wandered away, confused, as she still couldn't swallow, but sucked air through the hole in her throat. She saw the monstrous giant rise in front of the overturned bus. She knew it couldn't be real, but she ran anyway.

The Ratman seized her near the destruction of the package store and lifted her in the air. Pushed past the giant's lips, she was dragged down through the pile of rats packed inside. In the darkness and the hot stink of filth, Agnes tried to scream, but could only draw air in and out of the opening that kept her alive a little while longer.

The heat was unbearable the deeper she sank inside.

The first several rats were bloated and full. They nipped at her, but couldn't take another bite. Once she was deep enough inside the mass of rodents, the hungry rats reached her and started their work in earnest. They tore her apart quickly and one rat opened her breathing hole wider to begin working from the inside out.

She tried to grab for something to hold onto out of instinct. She kept grabbing rats that simply tore flesh from her hands in response. Finally, she grabbed the leg bone of the bus driver. Agnes held onto that until it was all over.

Roxie would eventually crawl out of the bus, long after the Ratman took 52 south again, and she passed out in the gravel until rescue arrived. The Ratman took the pile of bones, clutched in one massive hand, until he could find some more barbed wire.

Authorities had no idea what to make of what they found, and Roxie's babbling about the Hand of God and talking rats did not help clarify matters, until other killings were discovered. Even then, the bus crash was never fully explained.

The Ratman left the highway and returned to the woods before Kingstree, and he drew closer to the coast, but at a southeastern angle that would bring him back home to the town of Butler. He did finally find his barbed wire to string the bones. These wouldn't be discovered until later, in the 80s, and added to the legend.

9

Tommy Rinder was wrong.

It was sweltering hot as they weaved their way out of the scrapyard. He was sure he was going to pass out on the side of the road before they got anywhere near a place to spend quarters. Then, Bobby and Spitz could toss rusty screws and broken bolt heads at Tommy's belly.

The temperature dropped fast, easily by a degree a mile. The sweat that coated him felt cold in the wind, and gooseflesh erupted over his arms more than once. The wind was to his face, but Tommy thought he could bike all the way to a Florida beach in this cool wind.

The temperature had actually dropped fifteen degrees by the time they pedaled across Ocean Front, in Fuller Beach. They straddled their bikes, side-by-side, and looked on in wonder. At first, the wind stung them with the particles of sand it picked up off the beach and blasted into their faces. But very quickly, the beach had been scoured by the strong winds until the hard-packed sand was all that was left. Tommy had been to the beach during high and low tides, at all times during the year. The ocean was so far out this time, that it was difficult to see the waves from the sidewalk. If he squinted, he could be looking out over a desert instead of a beach. A few fish flopped in their final moments, where they'd been stranded by the lowest of low tides.

Tommy had never seen anything like this. His father and his grandfather could have told him exactly what this meant, but both of them were out at the prison.

They turned south on the ocean side of the walk and headed toward the tourist traps. Before they arrived, they found all the action at the Food Lion grocery store, on the inland side. The parking lot was packed. People fought over buggies and spaces. They fought over bread and milk.

Someone pulled a gun and backed off a man trying to grab a cart behind a van before the family was done unloading it.

Tommy cursed and braced himself to see a man die. He pictured the poisoned rat in the scrapyard, with its belly leaking. He pictured the cabin decorated with barbed wire, animal bones, and his spare scout shirt.

Bobby laughed after Tommy cussed. "They're acting like it's about to snow or something."

A voice carried out from the parking lot. It was a man's voice, and deep. Tommy wasn't sure why that voice carried clearer than the rest of the commotion, but he heard it, and he remembered the words clearly because of what happened later. "It's the tornados that cause all the damage."

Tommy looked out across the wide beach and the receded ocean on the other side. You couldn't predict tornados, so what were these folks predicting?

"I think we should go back," Tommy said.

"You worried about snow, too?" Bobby asked.

Tommy shrugged. "Something's happening."

Silence followed that comment. Tommy didn't know it, even though he had kind of felt it, but the pressure had steadily dropped around them the whole time they were riding out here. Neither Bobby nor Spitz knew it either, but it added just enough to their unease to give them pause. They met eyes, looking for resolve in the other, but not seeing it. The drawn silence was enough to take any fight out of them, so even though Bobby had quarters, the three of them started the long ride home empty-handed.

Carter Rinder's foot was giving him hell. He was sure he could muscle through when he'd finally limped out to the car that morning, but now, as afternoon rolled on and he still had more than a couple hours left in his shift, his foot was sticky agony.

He found an alcove, back and away from the stairs, to sit down on a concrete edge that stuck out from the rest of the wall, here in the interior hall outside the Block C bars. A couple weeks ago, a guy who one of the gangs thought was a rat got his head cracked open on the edge where Carter now sat. This was a blind spot. One of many around the old prison design. Carter wanted a blind spot as he pulled off his boot with his teeth gritted.

Blocks C and D were open to the yard. Carter got assigned to A Block because they were shorthanded, but he'd slipped over here to get a moment.

A few trustees piddled along the other halls in their assigned jobs rolling laundry, collecting trash, and probably delivering contraband. Carter was great at sniffing out contraband. Convicts were terrible at hiding guilt and fear on their faces when they were doing something wrong. Carter figured the ones who didn't show their guilt on their faces, didn't get caught like these dummies.

After the boot popped off his swollen foot, Carter let out a quiet squeak of restrained pain. The noise escaping him made him angry to the point that tears glazed the corners of his eyes. They didn't escape from the guard's tear ducts, though. He was half sure he wasn't ever getting that boot back on his abused foot.

Spots of black, green, and yellow spread through the grey material of the sock over his wounds. He peeled the sock down off his pale, hairy calf. The tape around the bandage pads was rolled up from sweat and effusions. The putrid color soaked through the white coverings. As they folded away with the sock, strings of goo stretched out from the wounds. Air struck the open sores with a sharp bite of pain.

He turned his nose away from the sour cheesy smell that seemed to cover his mouth and nose like a warm, wet cloth.

Sweat beaded on his forehead and Carter felt overwhelmingly tired. His head pulsed thick and soupy, too.

"You probably got a fever, Guard Rinder. I can slip you some antibiotics from the infirmary."

Carter brought his glossy eyes up to see the prisoner leaning casually at the opening of the alcove. Dr. Elroy Martin was probably their most educated inmate, and maybe their most accomplished prisoner. One fellow down in solitary might have been a close second. Accomplished in terms of having once held his own pediatric practice in three counties, including an office out by Harper Medical Plaza, not a few miles from this very prison. Before he was caught, Elroy was being praised for preparing to open a second Rutledge County office, out by the Washington Street Medical Center, to help the poor kids in Union Neck. None of his poisonings had happened at Rutledge, as far as they knew. He was only convicted for three child killings, in a different county, but he made off-the-books house calls and, the going theory was, he had killed more than any other inmate Grinder State held, possibly more than even the priest, making him the most accomplished prisoner in that regard, too.

"You already got your glasses broken by trying to be clever with a Mexican, Prisoner Elroy." Carter shivered as he rolled his sock back up. "You come here talking bribes to me because you're hungry and want to swallow your teeth?"

"No disrespect intended, Guard Rinder," Elroy said, still leaning. "I know you do important work here, have a family to support, and no hurt foot is going to keep you from doing that. I appreciate you pulling that angry Mexican off of me, too … eventually."

Carter took several deep breaths and then pressed his swollen foot into the tight mouth of his boot, to a rush of pain. "Wasn't anything personal, Baby Killer. Folks from the state were visiting that day, so I had to save you that time."

"I appreciate it, just the same," Elroy said. "They don't let me dispense meds to patients, but they let me work up in the infirmary when they're shorthanded. This place is always shorthanded."

Carter shook as he felt like his foot was tearing apart. He wanted to crack wise with Dr. Martin again, but was in too much agony to say anything. He had to get his foot back into the boot, even if it killed him.

"I know the screws up top would force you to take time off, if they knew, and that isn't right," Elroy said. "Not fair to you, and all you do here every day."

Carter paused in his efforts. "Are you threatening me, Prisoner?"

"No," Elroy said. "Never. I respect you. Don't want the system to cheat you. Wouldn't be fair that they punish you for getting hurt, taking food out of the mouths of your kids."

Having Elroy Martin mention his kids made Carter feel slimier than his leaking foot. He redoubled his efforts to get his boot on and tears did escape the corner of one eye this time.

"No need to involve people who don't care about you enough to help you stay on the job," Elroy continued. "I can get you the meds you need to get better on your own. You can double check on what I hand you. You can check with someone in case my past makes you nervous, I mean. Then, you're better on your own, without losing your hard-earned money in the process."

Carter's toes popped past the turn of the boot's heel in a rush. He had to pause again as he waited for the tightness in his stomach to pass. "And what sort of leverage are you looking for over me for this, Baby Killer?"

Elroy shrugged. "You don't owe me anything. I would never say anything to anyone anyway. I'm a lot of things, but I'm no rat. Maybe if someone jumps me again and there's no one from the state visiting that day, you'd pull them off of me anyway … eventually."

Carter braced himself and got his boot the rest of the way on. Elroy watched as Carter stood while holding the wall. He put weight on his foot slowly and limped forward. He had to work through the pain enough so that he could walk, and even jog a little if trouble started, without anyone noticing. Guards didn't tell on each other, but they also didn't want to get killed because the guy watching their back was a cripple.

"You'd take care of me?" Carter took a moment to smooth down the long bars of his mustache after he spoke.

Elroy stood up straight at the mouth of the alcove. "Whatever you need, Guard."

"Wouldn't poison me like those black babies you did in?"

"I was framed," Elroy said, "but I've also gotten my head right since then."

"You sure it's right, Prisoner?"

"Right as rain, Guard Rinder."

"Mmm." Carter bobbed his head and peeked out into the hall from the alcove. "Okay, here's what I need, Dr. Martin. I need you to listen close and understand exactly how this is going to work."

Elroy leaned in as the guard paused. Carter swung up from his hip with the billy club. He caught Elroy on the skin between his nose and his upper lip. He didn't knock out any teeth, but bounced Elroy's head off the wall and sent him to the floor.

Carter let go of the wall and leaned his weight on his bad foot, to work through the pain enough to fake the last hours of his shift.

Once he was confident he had it together again, he raised the club above Elroy on the floor.

"Carter, everything okay?" Assistant Warden Buck Spencer asked. He was a broad-shouldered, stocky man. Looked like they didn't design shirts and ties to fit him, but the man wore them anyway.

Carter lowered his club and looked down at Elroy on the floor. "Right as rain, Warden Spencer. What can I do you for?"

"Was he after you?"

Carter glanced down and back up. "Cornered me and started making demands, but I think Dr. Baby Killer has his head right again, don't you?"

Carter toed the man's ribs with his bad foot and regretted it.

"Yes, sir," Elroy said into the floor, without getting up.

Spencer shook his head. "There's a storm coming."

"Do we need to get everyone in from the yard?"

"It's being done now," Spencer said. "It's a bad one though. Your shift's going to have to stay on through the night, as back-up for night shift. We'll set up cots in the admin area so folks can rest when they're not on."

"Oh, come on," Carter held his back and looked up at the ceiling. He was tempted to show his foot so he could go home.

"I know. It's time and a half, though. I still got to tell a few others. Get this prisoner squared away in the hole, and then join back up getting the blocks locked down."

"What? The hole?"

Spencer tilted his head. "This prisoner threatened a

guard. He goes to solitary. Make it quick, though."

"I'll need to call my wife."

"Then get this prisoner squared away quick, Carter" Spencer said. "Warden Hendricks is up in Myrtle Beach for family stuff. I need this place airtight, so I don't get my tail in a sling when he gets back."

Warden Spencer left without waiting for an answer.

Carter dragged Elroy to his feet. "Come on. You keep your mouth shut, Dr. Death, or you'll wish I'd let that Mexican finish you off."

10

The Ratman wouldn't have come within sight of the coast until almost daylight the next morning, if he had walked straight to Butler as his dead senses and primal instincts for vengeance drove him to do, but something unusual detoured him to the east, buying Rutledge County and Tommy Rinder's family a few more precious hours that might have changed everything.

Ratman heard the voices of the creatures crying out to him. They were hungry, held captive, and neglected. There were enough of them putting out enough negative energy that felt to Ratman like broken promises.

He hated the Rinders, at this point, with a dark malignancy that matched his seventy-foot size. The draw from the east confused those senses and, like birds being turned around in their migration, the monster followed that new magnetic pole of dark energy to Chester Reptile House and Gator Farm.

Newt Chester lived in the backroom of the Reptile House. It was a cramped place, full of aquariums and serpents. Lizards, snakes, and other reptiles languished in improper temperatures and filthy habitats.

Next door, the alligators and crocodiles cruised around the overcrowded ponds within their fences, snapping at each other as they found nothing to eat.

Newt's place had been taken off the field trip rotation with most of the school systems around the area because of the incident last spring. It had taken a while to get the big snake to unlatch from the kid's shoulder, but he'd only bled a little, and it wasn't one of the venomous snakes. Still, bad press was bad press, so he'd cut back on the feeding budget just a little. Most of those things didn't need to eat as often as he was feeding them anyway.

It was hot that night and Newt opened his windows, laying on top of the sheets in nothing but his tightie-whities.

The ground rumbled in a steady pattern. The glass of the aquariums in the next room rattled, along with the light fixtures. Newt thought it was trucks going by, but then it got louder and sounded like impacts. Were they blasting somewhere? In the middle of the night?

He grabbed his pack of Marlboros and a lighter with the Confederate flag on it in the dark. He walked past the dark tanks. A number of the heat lamp bulbs had burned out, but those things were expensive. This summer was hot as Hades, anyway.

Newt unlocked and stepped out. He was fine with smoking in the building. The walls were stained with nicotine from when his dad and brother used to run the place. Only the animal smells covered up the smoke smells. He wanted relief though.

The wind off the ocean was vicious tonight. It cooled him down in a hurry, out there in nothing except his briefs, but he couldn't get his cigarette lit. He moved around the side of the building, cursing the whole way as gravel and sweetgum tree gumballs bit into his bare feet.

He never did get it lit.

As the roof tore off the house, he dropped to his knees and covered his head, thinking it had to be a tornado. There was supposed to be a still and eerie calm before those hit, he thought. He choked as he bit his unlit smoke in half and swallowed the filter.

Ratman had never asked his subjects to do something as complex as run in and open cages. It was a messy process. He only sent out a few from within him to do the job. Many of the snakes lashed out and struck the rats who had freed them. The rats, some of whom were as large as the biggest ones found in any New York sewer at that point, fought back, tearing the snakes' guts out of their scaly sides.

Their king was inclined to let them work out their differences until the survivors answered his call to return to him, adding to his power. Everyone needed to feed, after all.

Ratman busied himself tearing down the fences to set the gators free, as Newt wretched a couple more times, without bringing anything up.

Newt Chester confused the shape of the Ratman towering over him as the tornado. He watched in wonder as the wind from the ocean beat against his bare back. He waited to be taken off to Oz or to Hell.

As he spotted the gators racing across the ground toward him in the dark, he decided it must be Hell. During every show, he tossed plucked chickens into their dinosaur mouths and then told the crowd of passing tourists that an alligator could outrun a man over short distances. He also told them that crocodiles would attack a human no matter what, but alligators typically only approached people once humans had fed them because they then saw people as a source of food.

Even armed with that memorized knowledge, Newt tried to run away, but only managed to hobble over the sharp bits on the ground. As the monsters dragged him down and then fought over his limbs, he felt betrayed, because he was the one who had fed them.

As alligators tore meat away from Newt's ribs, his body weakened enough that his arms and legs separated. Then, the gators fought over those pieces, too. A large and scarred croc, known as Old Alice, swallowed Newt's head whole and did so unchallenged by the others.

Ratman called his creatures back to him. He knelt and rested his flexible chin on the ground so the crocs and gators could climb into his mouth. Old Alice required a boost from one of Ratman's massive hands. The rats inside his fist shifted to work the old crocodile between the Ratman's lips.

He stood and tore down one of the walls of the Chester Reptile House. Empty aquariums shattered inside. That was enough fighting. It was time to go. The surviving snakes and rats climbed back into their king's body.

He turned south and followed Highway 17 toward Rutledge County. Opening the cave of his mouth, the Ratman received bats battling the strong winds to reach him.

The sun would rise and more traffic would spot the hundred foot tall Ratman. They'd run off the road and find payphones to report the monster.

Police wouldn't challenge the giant until after the attack on the zoo, and just before it crossed the county line.

The next morning, emergency vehicles responding to the Reptile House thought it was a tornado, too, just as Newt had, before he was eaten. One of the volunteer firefighters picked a rebel flag lighter off the ground and kept it.

About the same time Rutledge County was torn apart by a rampaging giant, the agencies farther north of Fuller Beach put out a warning about escaped alligators. There was a lot more chaos going on along the coast by that point, though.

11

Tommy had gotten home before his father and rushed out to fix the swing for his sisters in the high winds that had finally reached Butler. More than once, a gale threatened to rip him right off the branch where he worked the knots he'd learned in Scouts. He felt like he might get lifted away like Superman, but he suspected he'd just fall on his head and break his neck, like his mother always said he was going to do one day.

When his sisters ran out to tell him that Daddy had to stay at the prison all night, Tommy felt a sense of relief. He took his time and finished the swing before coming inside.

Cloud cover had turned the sky dark before the sun set, as Tommy returned inside with his hair twisted around like a troll doll.

His sense of relief left him when he saw how uneasy

Mom was about a storm so bad Dad had to man the prison all night.

"He'll be fine," Tommy said weakly, over their quiet dinner.

She didn't look at him when she said, "Storms make animals and men stupid and crazy."

* * *

Carter Rinder got Elroy Martin stripped down, hosed down, and locked away in one of the cells in solitary. Once the good doctor was squared away in a dark box, Carter wandered over to cell fourteen. That was one year older than Carter's son, but the man in there had been locked up in that cell since Tommy was five years younger than that.

He opened the heavy food hatch and propped it up on its hinges. It would hold open as it was designed to do, wide enough to pass food inside on the shelf for the prisoner, but the slightest touch would bring the metal hatch slamming closed with crushing weight. It was meant to slam closed on prisoners grabbing a guard but, in practice, it was the guards' wrists that usually got slammed, sometimes hard enough to cause a fracture.

The worst offenders, ones who had gone batty from too much time alone with their own diseased thoughts, tried to bite with their diseased mouths or throw collected wastes on the people trying to feed their ungrateful gobs.

Carter didn't fear this prisoner was going to do any of that, but maybe he should have.

The voice out of the darkness croaked, "That you, Carter?"

"Yeah, Dad," Guard Carter Rinder answered the prisoner.

Zell Rinder shifted in the darkness of cell fourteen and drew closer to the open feeding slot. There wasn't much light out here from the high windows in this section. From Zell's perspective, it was blindingly bright.

If Carter had ever seen the narrow spaces between cars at the scrapyard his son traveled, it would have reminded him very much of this canyon of concrete that was solitary in the Grinder. He knew it was partially underground because the concrete leaked steadily below a certain line on the walls. Digging into the ground in South Carolina, and this close to the coast, was stupid. They had to have known that in the 30s, when they started this project. Maybe it was the same logic that made the walls here needlessly high.

Zell finished his shuffling and his son Carter pictured the old man in there, hunched over, barely picking up his feet anymore. He skittered toward the light like some animal in its burrow. Some man-rat coming out to check for its shadow.

Sixty more years of winter, you cop-killing screw-up.

A howl rose from cell seven, across and down, to the left. It spiraled up and echoed through the odd, wet space of solitary. It brought Carter up out of his thoughts and then it was done. He had a right to yell for the prisoner to be silent. He could risk opening the hatch and spraying a hose inside. He could open the door and go in with just his club to teach the ex-priest a lesson. None of those things were going to silence Alias Orwell. The old monster thought he was possessed by a legion of demons, and Carter was inclined to give him the benefit of the doubt.

The hasp that latched over Alias Orwell's feeding slot hatch was getting loose from all the years he'd been down there. Carter had no way of knowing that, or seeing it from this distance in the low light.

"Going into lockdown for the storm," Carter said.

"I'm always in lockdown," his father said.

Because you deserve it, Rat.

"Went camping with the boy this weekend," Carter said. It sounded stupid coming out of his mouth, all ordinary, in a place like this.

"Up in the mountains?"

Carter nodded, without thinking about how stupid that was, leaning outside his father's cell. "Out by the Ironheel Creek … western side, of course."

"Tell the boy?"

"Tell him what?"

Carter knew that would get under the old man's skin. The old rat had raised a hand to Carter for no account enough times that screwing with his head was a small thing in comparison.

81

"Come on now. You still keeping the promise, ain't you?"

"Was it Mace Finch, Dad?"

"What's this about now?"

"Who sent you up to Conway for that heist with the Elvis boys? What got Old Man Elvis killed, and that cop? It was a Finch job you were completing, wasn't it?"

"I never killed that cop. You know that. Everyone knows that."

"Driving away the guy who did it was no better, was it?"

"Didn't kill anyone, boy. Wrong place. Wrong life, is all."

"You didn't answer my question, Dad."

"You didn't answer mine, neither," Zell said. "Your question don't matter, and can't be answered. Mine does, and needs to be."

"If it was so damn important to feed some imaginary monster," Carter said, "you should have been doing that instead of robbing Mace Finch's rivals and chauffeuring cop killers."

"Did you keep the promise or not?"

Carter huffed in a way that didn't quite rise to the level of a real laugh. "I went for a while. Every week, like the old days. Kind of the way a kid keeps praying after he's grown because his daddy made him think the Devil would come and get him if he slipped on the incantations and genuflections."

"The Ratman is real. I've seen him. My daddy seen him."

Carter turned his head down and to the side, in the direction of the open hatch. "Well, I never did, because there was never anything to see, old man."

"How long ago did you break the promise, Carter?"

Carter sighed and looked away from the slot. "Tapered off, really. I'd have a bad dream and head up there. Go through the motions like before. Sort of playing at the old religion of my fathers. The scout trip out there was just a coincidence. I wasn't even planning to go this time, but when I found out where they were going, it sort of felt like a sign. I went and took the boy up to see the cabin, past the ruins of Gomorrah."

"Good," Zell almost sounded joyful. "Good. If you keep up the promise again, and pass it on to the boy after you, it may not be too late to save us all."

"You live in a dark box. You see the sun once a week, from the bottom of a concrete pit, with a cage over the top in case rats learn how to fly."

Zell's voice came harsh from between what remained of his yellow teeth. "I ain't no rat."

"You ain't no man, either."

"I'm in this box on account of you, boy. Nothing keeping me here, except you. Just let me go to a regular cell with a window. Eat my meals on a seat at a table."

"You'd be dead before you got a chance to sit down, you old fool. Most scumbags don't know you're here, and the moment they do, they'd kill you for sharing my last name. So, you're staying put for however long you go on creeping the Earth."

"You don't care whether I live or die," Zell said. "Let me die in the sun, fighting, then."

"This ain't about you, Ratman." Carter gave a couple huffs, closer to a real laugh. "I barely started working here when you got sent up. Then, you landed here, probably because your old buddy Mace wanted you close in case you needed killing. I'm not having trouble start up around you where the wardens can tie that trouble to me. You screwed up my life enough when you were free. Now, you can rot away in peace and quiet. It's been a great visit. Talk to you soon."

Carter reached for the hatch.

"Just keep up the promise."

Carter closed his fist as he paused for a few seconds. He shifted his weight onto his bad leg and showed his teeth from the dirty pain. "Listen, I didn't pass this nonsense on to my son like you did me. I told him the story. Made it into a real spook story, but made sure it was the bad joke it has always been. The old god of my fathers is a pile of rats, inside the skin of a man. This family has been worshipping a made-up demon for generations. The Rinders are the biggest idiots in Rutledge County for it."

Orwell howled from seven again. The hasp on cell seven lost its grip on the side of the feeding hatch and fell away. There's no way the priest could have known this had happened, but he did anyway. Same way he knew a storm was coming, and something darker than that right behind it.

Zell shouted over the priest, "Tell me you kept the promise! Tell me you fed him."

A door opened on the end of the solitary block and footsteps approached.

Carter pitched his voice low. "I left that empty cabin where it lay for the last time, and made sure my son wouldn't never go back."

"You're going to get us all killed for breaking that promise. We're all going to pay."

"Wasn't ever my promise," Carter said. "You're the one paying for broken promises, Ratman."

Carter slammed the hatch with a crash and thumbed the hasp into place to latch it closed. It felt a little loose to him, but he supposed everything around here was showing its age.

An older guard named Filmore shuffled past, with keys jingling on his belt. The keys didn't bother Carter, but the raspy sound of the man's feet echoing back from the high walls made his skin crawl.

"You dropping one off, Rinder?"

Carter passed Filmore without breaking stride. "Put Baby Killer Elroy Martin in down on the end. Maybe you forget he's there until he turns skeleton?"

Filmore chuckled. He noticed Carter Rinder had a slight limp, but decided not to mention it. The inmates down here had nothing to do but listen. Best not to let them hear anything. "I'll thin him up a little on bread and water for you. You stuck here for the storm?"

Carter let himself out of solitary. "We're all prisoners now, huh?"

"Sure enough."

The door was closed and Carter gone before Filmore had answered.

The lone guard paused on his way down to give Doctor Baby Killer the orientation lecture. He bent at the waist to retie his shoe.

When he was younger, he had delivered it like a drill sergeant. The words had lost some passion as the decades wore on. Now, he just stated the rules and the consequences as matters of fact. These men were yelled at all the time and mostly numb to it. Filmore found talking to them quiet and dry tended to break their spirits quicker. It resigned them to the reality, he thought, maybe.

He stood up straight and thought about his late wife Abigail for the last time. He'd never mentioned her while inside the prison. He let the inmates think he was a bachelor, with no attachments and nothing to lose. They were more likely to kill the guy telling about his kids as he begged for his life, Filmore theorized. They wanted to take something away from people who took away from them.

Filmore wasn't going to show them anything worth taking, he thought, as the hatch on seven, right next to him, burst open from the inside the way it wasn't supposed to. Orwell seized Filmore's belt and pulled him against the door, with the hatch digging into his spine.

Filmore screamed for help as the wind and rain really picked up outside. Orwell took the keys and used a few of them in his fist to punch the guard in the kidneys, stabbing him through the back multiple times.

As blood spread across the back of his uniform, other inmates started screaming and yelling. Orwell heard none of it. Even his own voices had gone quiet as he carried out their previous instructions. He'd tried for years to resist them, to exorcise them himself, but some demons don't come out, even with prayer and fasting.

He liked Filmore, too. Genuinely liked him.

Filmore tried to draw his club, but dropped it with a clatter as the feeling went out of his arms. After the weight went dead, Orwell let go of the belt and allowed the guard to drop. In the time it took him to figure out the right key, feeling for the lock through the feeding slot, Filmore had finished dying.

Solitary had gone quiet again, as Orwell had to fight the dead guard's weight along the floor enough to push the door open and slip out.

Orwell tracked blood a few steps with bare feet. Then he turned his attention to Filmore's shoes and socks. The guard wasn't going to need them. Filmore's Abby wasn't going to miss him anymore, either, so this was a good thing. That's what the voices told him.

On the other end of solitary, Doctor Elroy Martin had listened to everything since he got here. He learned about Carter Rinder and his father. He heard Filmore die, screaming for Orwell to have mercy, even over the other inmates. He heard the door open after everyone went quiet again.

With a swollen lip, he called, "Father Orwell, let me out, too."

All the inmates started yelling again as rain sheeted outside and water seeped down the interior walls of the cells. Alias Orwell untied the dead guard's shoes without hearing any of it.

The doctor was going to have to figure out something else.

12

If Valarie Kemper had heard that Newt Chester, of the Chester Reptile House and Gator Farm, had died, she wouldn't have even bothered to pretend to be civil or Christian about it. She'd have smiled or even laughed. The last Chester was gone.

She'd toasted the death of Newt's father with two six packs of 16 ounce King Cobra Malt Liquor black cans. She'd felt like she was dying in her trailer behind the Swamp Fox Zoo, off Highway 17, the next morning, but it had been worth it.

When Gordon Chester went to Grinder State Prison for robbing gas stations, she had a free day at the zoo. When he died of some lung infection inside, she bought eight tall bottles of B-40 Bull Max eight percent.

There's no way of knowing what she would have bought had she known Newt had died. She was drinking a lot of Olde English over that last month of her life. If she'd known he died in a tornado or eaten by his own gators, she might have sprung for some local craft beer or something with the word ale in the name.

Swamp Fox Zoo had no permits, and the bars on the cages weren't very strong. The Ratman tore right through them. Half the animals climbed into his mouth with mesmerized obedience. A few of the bigger cats burst into the trailer and dragged her out screaming.

She still thought it was a nightmare she could wake up from as Ratman palmed her and the cats down his throat, to share her with the rats, gators, and bats he'd picked up on his way south.

* * *

The Rutledge Sheriff, Tammy Hucks Rinder's distant relation, along with the Fuller Beach and Butler police, had mobilized for the storm coming in. They were all on duty when state patrol officers drove out in the early morning to investigate the wild tales of monsters on the highway.

The first two officers lasted long enough to fire their weapons up into the two hundred foot tall giant, reload, fire again, call for back-up in a frantic message that sounded like a call from a war zone, and reloaded again.

The Ratman crushed their vehicle flat enough to stack in the scrapyard, but then hurled it three miles out into the ocean. One officer broke his leg. His partner tried to drag him away screaming, but then the rats and Old Alice were released on them and they both died screaming.

While the Ratman was still hanging their bones from the power lines, deputies from the county immediately north of Rutledge and more highway patrol arrived in separate waves. They had no time to mount an organized defense.

Each shot they fired punched through the skin, stretched to its limit. Every rat, snake, and creature in the path of the bullets took mortal wounds until the power behind the bullets was absorbed and stopped. The torn skin moved and pulsed as the other creatures inside fed on the dying and wounded animals in the path of the bullet. This served to enrage Ratman.

He destroyed their vehicles, and tore the men out of the metal if they tried to hide inside. He lost patience with trying to collect their bones, so he tore them apart in his rat-filled hands. Some of the pieces he swallowed, to add to the feast. Others, he threw aside for people to try to make sense of later.

Tuesday morning was warming up, and the wind and rain from the tropical depression that had missed the Carolina coast was looping back out to sea. Ratman was on his way back home to the county where Sully Rinder had been born.

Sheriff Hucks had heard the first message from the highway patrol radio. He thought maybe those boys had been caught out in a flash flood as they called for help. He said a little prayer for them as he positioned his men and the joint task force to handle rescue, and possibly looters, in Rutledge.

When the rest of the calls came in over the top of each other, he knew something else was going on. The words and descriptions didn't make sense. Even good men could be overcome by fear when fighting for their lives. He heard gunfire before radios cut off. You didn't shoot hurricanes unless you were some drugged-out white trash lowlife on a bender.

Hucks was good at paying attention, though. It was something that had kept him alive while dealing with thugs. It kept him alive in election years, when he was challenged. Through the panicked cries for help, he picked up street names, store locations, and mile markers as they came through. The group attacking the highway patrol and county law enforcement, immediately north of Rutledge, was traveling down 17 to where it became Ocean Front, and they were coming his way.

The storm wasn't much compared to what people had feared it would be. It was summer, so no school to cancel. A few power lines were down, but utilities were already moving and they never moved until the storm had passed. A few fallen trees that citizens were moving off the road their own selves. A lot of small limbs and trash that needed cleaning up, but nothing to justify every shift being on. Nothing, until the highway patrol went to war up the road.

Sheriff Hucks switched gears from storm prep to riot control. He retained command of all the forces. He informed of the new threat, setting up units around the county where they could be called in if needed. Then, he put himself and most of the combined forces out on the northern county line, blocking off Ocean Front.

Whoever was moving in on them was going to surrender short of Rutledge, or get cut apart and sent to Hell before they succeeded in crossing the line.

When he saw the giant lumber into view, it locked him up. It was in the shape of a man, but stretched and sagged like something built for a movie set in a hurry. The ground shook with each heavy step, and the thing covered several feet of ground with each casual stride. Through fissures in the rubbery skin, Hucks would have sworn later that he saw things moving in there, and glowing eyes staring out at him.

Soon, he'd find out.

The eyes of the giant monster were empty pits. There was nothing behind them, no life within them, except for writhing shadow. The mouth hung open and flapped with the ocean winds and the impact of each thundering step. It looked as if the monster was mumbling to itself, with a black screen of baleen behind its lips instead of teeth. And more red eyes staring out from the flapping maw of this godless terror.

The stretching and roiling skin bothering him the most. The uncanny strangeness of it made his own skin crawl. It looked fake, but in the way the skin of decomposing corpses left out in the woods to be found by the law looked unreal. This was like the stretched skin of a giant dead man stalking toward him. Instead of bone, this walking ghoul was filled with two hundred feet of dark evil.

It froze Sheriff Hucks up, but only for a moment. There was no denying that the patrols on the dying radios had faced something horrific, and this fit the bill, if not the rules of the natural world. Every cop had stories that bordered on the supernatural, or brought into question God's creation. Nothing like this, but this was the threat before them now, and he wasn't going to go down screaming into his radio.

The men were starting to back away. That wouldn't do.

"Hold your ground," Hucks yelled. They hesitated, but continued to edge a retreat. "I said stand your ground, men. We stop this thing, here and now, or we let it in to attack our families and kill our children. We stop it here. It does not enter Rutledge County. I will not allow it."

Hucks drew his sidearm and brought the rifle off his back onto the hood of his cruiser. Other men exchanged looks. They all saw fear in each other's eyes, but none of them wanted the other to see a coward. Some of them exchanged handguns for shotguns, but they all squared up behind the cover of the cars and the barricades, for what it was worth.

The Ratman closed the distance in proportion to his

height.

"Let him have it," Hucks ordered. "Center mass and headshots. Don't stop until it does."

The world erupted in gunfire. They hardly had to aim to achieve shots to the body and head. The flesh rippled like a sheet in the wind with all the impacts. Sometimes holes were too small to see. Other times they caused the stretched skin to split open in wide wounds. Smoke rose in tendrils from areas of the body and head that were hit more than once in a row.

Hucks was good with details and he noticed the beast was still coming and lifting its misshapen arms to reach for them. Its gait was unnatural. It wasn't like muscle movement. It was shifting, like a toddler learning to walk, compensating just in time to keep it from tipping over. For some reason, he pictured a cartoon, with cats putting on a human costume to sneak into a store to buy milk.

The monster bled dark out of the open wounds, but it didn't fall or falter in its wobbling charge. The dark blood didn't flow. It crawled down the flesh, toward the ground. Hucks mentally compared it to a swarm of insects.

Through the wind, he heard something like words. Even through the gunfire, it sounded like the monster was speaking in a hissing voice.

The ocean winds swept away the blueish-grey smoke above the officers' heads, but the endless fire continued to create a new cloud around them.

This was contagious fire. He had set them loose with the order to keep shooting until the monster fell, and they would. They'd be deaf and still firing, as this creature that was bleeding black insects stepped on top of them.

Hucks waited another couple seconds and got his opening. Enough of them were reloading that he could throw in another command. If he had said for them to hold their fire, it would have never happened. He could try something else that might work.

"Aim for the legs. Cut off its legs and bring it down."

That order got relayed.

"Legs!"

"Shoot out its legs."

"… cut out from under it …"

The gunfire redoubled as the men grabbed onto any hope they could take. At first, there was very little difference. More bullets missed, but even the ones that hit didn't appear to be having any effect. Then, the flesh tore and more dark blood crawled out and joined what was spreading across the street.

The monster drew close enough for the shotguns to start having an impact, instead of just making noise. That was too close.

Then, Hucks noticed another detail.

Rats? Are those rats coming toward us from its body?!

A number of the men had stopped firing and were backing away. The rats washed across the ground toward the barricades, like a plague.

97

"Fall back," Hucks yelled. If they were going to do it anyway, he might as well make it an order to avoid any confusion. "Fall back."

The men were happy to follow this order, too.

Ratman dropped to his damaged knees and then his massive, misshapen hands smashed through wooden sawhorses and orange barrels as they planted on the street. One of the crushed barrels popped out from under the fingers and shattered the windows on one of the closest cruisers.

Even with the sheriff's ears ringing, to the point that he thought one of them might be bleeding, he heard the Ratman breath out a clear word. Just as his walking looked like a giant toddler learning to balance, this word came like some alien beast learning to speak. It sounded, for all the world, to him, like hundreds of animals imitating human speech all at once.

The rats, staring out of their king's lips with red eyes glowing, said, "Feed."

Then, they poured out of his head to obey.

The officers piled into cars together and whoever found himself behind the wheel drove everyone inside away, as fast as he could. Hucks jammed his vehicle into reverse with mostly Butler police in the front and back. He raced backward, kicking up sand and gravel the whole way, with two of his wheels tearing along the shoulder of the road.

As the rats flowed out of the Ratman's skin, a few remaining bones from a bus driver, Agnes' skeleton,

Valarie Kemper's bones, and random bones from a few officers who died north of the Rutledge line, spilled out onto the street around the wheels of the cruisers.

Hucks reached the first road leading west, into the county, and away from the ocean. In the moment he took to shift into drive again, other cars from the various agencies barreled past him. Most decided to roar along Ocean Front a little farther, to get as far from this abomination as possible.

A number of vehicles were abandoned and now coated with a blanket of filthy rats. They fought their way through windows still rolled down just an inch or so. The rodents flattened their bodies in a boneless way to squeeze inside.

Looking for us ... looking for people to ... feed on.

The rats spread out on both sides of the road. They scurried through the tall grass, toward the beach houses on the inland side of the road. They climbed the sheer concrete walls of a resort on the beach, just inside Rutledge County.

"All those people," Hucks said. "We didn't save anyone."

The guys who were crowded in the front seat heard him, but didn't respond.

"Gators," one of the guys in the back said.

A lion? Hucks thought, as he squinted through the windshield.

The nonsensical ark of animals moved down the street toward the sheriff's cruiser, as the other men had long left the scene.

Beyond the overwhelmed cars, the monster's emptied body billowed on the ground. The wind off the ocean, still strong from the edges of the storm out at sea, blew through the holes in the flesh. The stretched skin reminded Hucks of a parachute on the ground.

Was this their chance to destroy whatever this was? Had they already destroyed it? What the hell were they supposed to do with all these animals?

He considered staying to try to round up the bigger creatures. The rats would require months of traps and poison. They might never get rid of them all. Fuller Beach might become like New Orleans, where rats were just a way of life, as Hucks understood it down there.

He hesitated a moment longer, with the tension of the other officers in the vehicle growing into something that could almost be felt on a psychic level. Hucks reached to shift into drive, but realized he'd already done so. He drove west, back toward Butler, and radioed for animal control.

There was no way to conspire to keep a secret like this. Too many people saw it. The officers of Rutledge sort of decided, each on his own, to keep the horrors to himself in the same way old men didn't used to talk about war except with each other. Every cop had stories that bordered on the supernatural, or brought into question God's Creation. Ratman was bigger than all that. The stories were eventually told, after enough time had passed that it was safe to doubt again.

A number of rats followed west behind the car. After several minutes, the rats stopped and turned back the way they had come.

Tourists, who hadn't left town ahead of the forecasted storm, were caught by surprise when rats filled their rooms. Some lay dead or still dying. Others stared in shock as the plague left as quickly as it had begun. Their rooms lay coated in blood and droppings.

Along the beach, the more stubborn vacationers, who had stayed out the storm and returned to the hard sands, even as the winds continued and the red warning flags remained up, now ran south away from the rats and alligators chasing them. Even though the windblown sand was more compact, they learned how hard it was to run full-out in sand. Their knees hurt, shins ached, backs cramped, and the weight they had failed to put off in the spring caught up to them as they ran for their lives and heaved for breath.

When the rats and other creatures gave up the chase in unison, many of the survivors, some of them holding their children under their arms, collapsed where they stood.

Along the sand, rats that had taken wounds during the firefight were chewed on by their fellows. The carcasses were left where they lay until the tide finally came in later that day and washed the dead away.

On Ocean Front, at the county line, Ratman filled with all manner of creatures. Things with wings, things with fur, things with scales, and more crawled back inside all the holes around the skin until he regained his consciousness.

It took a long time for him to figure out a configuration that worked. With all the holes torn in him, especially around the legs, animals kept falling out and he had to start over, arranging them.

Finally, he stood to a height a few feet shorter than when he had arrived. The rats and reptiles in his legs bit onto one another's bodies and tails to keep from falling out through the tears in their master's skin. They twisted and contorted their bodies as they held on with their teeth to give him strength.

Ratman took out his rage on the abandoned cars, crushing them, tearing them apart, rolling them out to the water's edge, and hurling sharp pieces of metal so that they slipped like stones out to sea.

All of this gave Tommy and his friends time to assemble. It was Tommy Rinder who the Ratman sensed first that morning, and he stalked forward on his strange legs, along Ocean Front, to make the boy pay the price for broken promises.

13

"I can't believe they made your father stay all night in that place for a little wind," Mom said, as she cleared the kids' plates from breakfast. "He should get a raise and overtime. The monsters he has to …"

The kitchen phone rang. Tommy startled as the plates crashed in the sink and Mom nearly tore the phone off the wall. The cord was all tangled, so she had to lean over. "Hello? Hello? I'm here."

She frowned and took the phone away from her ear as she fought the tangles like she was trying to kill a snake. "It's one of your friends, Tommy. Get off the line quick, in case your father calls."

She got enough of the cord freed that Tommy could accept the receiver from over the counter.

He listened to Spitz and then said, "Okay, I'll ask … Mom, Shawn says Bobby King's family could use help down at their place from the storm."

She stared at him a moment. "It was a tropical depression. Didn't even get named. Didn't come onto shore, according to the radio. We never lost power."

"They did," Tommy said. "They're closer to the beach."

"You aren't a contractor, Tommy."

He frowned. "I am a good friend, though. I can help move the small branches and clean up the parking lot for their motel. That's what neighbors do, right?"

She sighed. "Fine. Don't go near any downed power lines."

"She said, yes." Tommy leaned over the counter to hang up the phone.

Holly Anne said, "The swing's down again."

"Yeah, don't make us tell Dad you didn't fix it." Ashley stuck out her tongue.

"I did fix it yesterday."

"Well, it isn't fixed now." Holly Anne stuck out her tongue.

"Just fix the swing first," Mom said. "You're concerned about being a good friend and neighbor. Be a good brother, too."

"Yeah, be a good brother for once," Ashley said, in a singsong voice.

"Yeah, for once," Holly Anne echoed.

Mom, of course, didn't seem to think their sarcasm and being bad sisters needed to be called out.

Tommy felt like he was always late to everything

with his friends.

Before their mom left the room, Tommy said, "Okay, but I almost fell out of that tree yesterday, and there is still a lot of wind and the tree is wet today. What do you think, Mom?"

He stuck out his tongue at his sisters during the pause, while Mom's back was still turned.

***

As he rode away on his bike, without fixing the swing first, he stuck his tongue out at his sisters again, watching from the driveway. Ashley, standing behind their little sister, had stuck up her middle finger at Tommy. He laughed.

He met Spitz and Bobby at the Shady Palms Motel and leaned his bike next to the other two by the brick wall, on the southern end of the property. Bobby had gotten up to go riding, like normal, before his parents informed him he had work first. Like a real up and coming businessman, he'd recruited his two friends into the effort.

Bobby walked toward the curb with more palm fronds and thin pine branches. Spitz struggled with the leaves and debris pasted to the parking lot. Some of it had already turned black.

Bobby finished up what he'd been saying before Tommy arrived. " … so the boy wakes up in the hospital and sees the girl next to his bed. He asks her what happened and she said, I was playing with your toy soldier. He squirted me in the face, so I bit his head off."

Spitz actually laughed.

Tommy cut in. "Where are your folks?"

"They drove down to get some tarps," Bobby said, as he walked back from the curb. "The roof is leaking in three of the rooms."

Tommy wished he had worn jeans. This was the first time it had been below seventy degrees, during the day or night, all summer. With the wind still gusting around them, gooseflesh crawled over his skin.

"How clean do they want it?" Tommy picked up one flexible twig with green pine needles on the end.

"No matter how clean we make it," Bobby said, "they'll always find something wrong with it. Just keep going until they get back."

"I'm so glad you invited us along." Tommy twirled the pine twig, spinning the needles like a fan or a blade.

"At least they won't yell at me while you guys are here," Bobby said. "Once they get busy with the roof, they'll tell us to go away."

"You need help with that branch?" Spitz asked, as he walked toward the curb with an armload of dripping debris.

Tommy stuck up his middle finger and threw the twig at Spitz's back. "No, I got it. The parking lot looks clean enough to me."

"Lazier than your mother in the sack," Spitz said.

Bobby asked, "What's the difference between a

pregnant woman and a lightbulb?"

Spitz said, "You actually need more lightbulbs."

Bobby said, "You can unscrew a lightbulb."

Tommy asked, "What is long and hard and full of seaman?"

Both Spitz and Bobby answered, "A submarine."

Spitz added, "And your mom."

"Gotta learn some new ones," Bobby said.

"What do you call a lesbian dinosaur?" Spitz asked.

Bobby started laughing before Spitz could say the punchline.

Before Spitz could finish the joke, glass exploded out of the motel office area, on the northern end of the lot, as the roof flipped three times in the air. The front desk splintered and flew out of the obliterated office. The roof landed on top of the pieces of desk in the parking lot and broke apart.

Spitz dropped the wet branches and staggered backward with brown leaves pasted to his shirt. Bobby's mouth hung open as he stood frozen near Tommy, who backed away from the destruction with his arms over his head.

The brick walls bulged, then folded out in the middle, before they rolled out in chunks, like a wave of water washing across the debris-filled parking lot. This was followed by wooden siding, pink insulation, pipes, wires, and real water. Lamps, paintings, beds, and TVs rolled out of the rooms that were nearest the office.

Then, the balconies came down. The roof collapsed

and covered over all that. Pieces of furniture and structure from the second floor rooms spilled out from the impact.

Water geysered out and to the west from one corner of the fallen wing of the Shady Palms. Then, a toilet landed not ten feet in front of Tommy and Bobby, where it shattered with the sound of dropped plates.

Spitz ran past them, toward the bikes. Bobby looked back and forth between the destruction and his friends. Tommy just shook his head, until he saw the shape moving in the mushroom cloud of rising dust.

It was too big to be real.

Tornadoes create all the destruction …

The shadow resembled the shape of a giant man, but then shifted into something else. He imagined some terrible demon rising from Hell, and that wasn't really too far from the truth.

Ratman …

"Rinder," the voice that wasn't human issued from the dissipating cloud above the destroyed motel.

Tommy knew that couldn't be real, but Bobby froze in place again, too, at the sound. Whether it was really a voice speaking Tommy's name, Bobby heard something.

Ratman stepped across the smashed building and towered over the boys, one hundred and seventy feet tall.

"Promises," the creature hissed out, drawing out each syllable, almost too long to recognize the word.

109

Bobby screaming in one shrill note didn't make it any easier to hear.

Tommy would probably have died right there. Maybe his friends would have died, too, depending on whether Ratman simply crushed the son of Carter Rinder, grandson of Zell Rinder, or tossed him into his mouth to be chewed apart by the creatures inside his skin. Or if the Ratman unleashed all those creatures to clean the boys' bones before the monster went looking for barbed wire. Before any of that happened, though, Tommy saw the rips in the skin of the monster's legs. He saw the rats and other vermin linked together, tooth to tail. He saw them bending and twisted to the movement of the monster. That horror and disgust was enough to trigger the lingering fear and confusion from his father's "prank" on the camping trip, along with every detail of the story. The story, the cabin, the bones, the Ratman, and his shirt hanging up in there. *He doesn't like boys. I should have never brought you here.*

He didn't exactly connect all the details to know what was going on or why, but it was enough for him to sprint away, instead of just standing there waiting to die. Tommy's motion woke up Bobby, and he ran, too.

The three of them took up their bikes and pedaled like the Devil was chasing them. In a sense, this might have been worse than that.

Ratman turned, without walking to the end of the parking lot. He plowed into the main wing of the motel and broke the place in half. The rooms on his

110

right folded in on themselves, going down faster than the office had. The left side held a little longer. As the monster attempted to push through, he got hung up on some of the struts and supports in the building.

The boys picked up speed, escaping up the road to the west.

His rat legs started to come loose. He actually had to lean on the surviving roof to steady himself. Shingles pulled loose under his weight. Nails stabbed into the rats inside his palm. They squealed, but he didn't notice.

"Where do we go?" Bobby cried out, nearly breathless.

"If we get to my house, we can hide," Spitz said.

Ratman lifted his fists and smashed them down. Some of the animals inside him broke their backs with the force of the impacts. Others inside the skin fed upon the dead, but Ratman kept fighting himself loose. The building shifted. Supports snapped and a load-bearing wall twisted diagonally. The rest of the motel folded in on itself and Ratman trudged onward after his prey.

* * *

"What if it sees our bikes out there?" Bobby dropped to his knees in Spitz's living room, heaving for breath.

"What was that thing?" Spitz ignored Bobby's question. His desperate cry sounded like an accusation to Tommy.

Tommy shook his head. "I don't know. How am I supposed to know?"

111

"We need to go out and hide our bikes," Bobby said.

"I'm not going back out there," Tommy said.

Spitz held up his hands. "Just be quiet so it doesn't hear us."

Bobby and Tommy both nodded.

After a moment of silence, Spitz yelled out, "Mom? Dad?!"

Tommy and Bobby both shushed him.

"They must be at work," Spitz whispered.

Tommy dropped into a worn-out recliner.

"Was that thing really some kind of ..." Bobby bent over and held his stomach as an unhealthy belch escaped his throat.

"Don't throw up in my house," Spitz said. "My parents will murder me if you mess up the new carpet."

The front door thundered as it tore loose from the house, crashing inward with the frame still attached to the dislodged door by the lock and hinges.

The boys screamed.

A misshapen arm snaked inside and clawed onto the chair Tommy sat in. He tried to jump out of it, but it reclined and opened up, trapping him for a moment, as Ratman dragged it toward the doorway. He was almost outside before Tommy rolled out of it.

Tommy got splinters in his hand, but ignored them as he stood up to run.

"Rinder!"

They all heard it that time. Tommy could see it in his friends' eyes.

112

A second fist crashed through the front window and whipped around inside, feeling around for them.

14

In Grinder prison, guards retreated through the facility as the prisoners overturned tables in the cafeteria and used broken bunks to try to smash through the security doors between them and the outside of the cell blocks.

Disgraced doctor Elroy Martin stuck close to Alias Orwell. Prisoners attacked each other as old rivalries and unreconciled debts and offenses were collected upon in the absence of order and authority during the riot. The prisoners who knew Orwell, stayed clear. Those who didn't know him followed the lead of older prisoners, who acted like Orwell was a wild animal in their midst.

Orwell walked calmly, though. His half open eyes scanned the violence and death around him like he didn't see it, or it did not impress him. He held onto

114

the leash he had fashioned out of the late Guard Mark Filmore's belt, and pulled Zell Rinder along between himself and Elroy Martin.

Orwell had really liked Mark Filmore.

Elroy had to think fast back when he was still trapped down in solitary. There was no way he could have been heard over all those crazy inmates yelling for Orwell to let them go. He had to think. He had been the only one down there with advanced education, other than Alias Orwell himself. Most of these guys hadn't finished high school. Elroy had needed to be smart.

He had pitched his voice low, sure it wasn't going to work. He couldn't even get his food slot open. How was Orwell going to hear this? He had to try anyway. "Orwell, we want Elroy Martin released. Open his cell, last one on the end, for us. We need him to walk with you to fulfill our will."

Orwell had heard that voice under all the other noise. He had used the guard's keys to free Elroy, just as the voice had told him, and he had listened to Elroy when the doctor had told him they needed Zell Rinder, too.

In the midst of the morning riot that had unfolded, Zell shielded his eyes from the light he still wasn't used to, as his captors pulled him slowly along through all the chaos. He whispered, "Because we broke the promise."

Orwell heard that voice, too, but didn't understand its meaning or message.

★ ★ ★

The guards ran down the corridor, away from where the prisoners had broken through from Block B. Carter Rinder held the wall as the other guards rounded the corner ahead of him. He couldn't feel his foot anymore at all, but the pain radiated up his leg. He felt it in his bones every time he took a step.

The prisoners moved toward his position with a roar he could hear and feel before they were even within sight.

He heard the security doors slam and lock around the corner, ahead of him. It was like being closed in his tomb before he was dead. They would not open them, no matter how much he beat on them, and these degenerates would have him.

What they would do to him …

He thought about the story of Sully, the Ratman.

Carter moved forward in a stumbling gait, but then cut to the right, into one of the alcoves near a stairwell. He could have taken the stairs, but he would still be locked in here, and probably run into another mob eventually. Instead, he found a dark corner, deep in a blind spot, and pulled his legs against his chest like he was some little kid hiding from monsters.

As Carter's bad foot throbbed in time with his heart, the mob stampeded past his hiding place. Shadows flickered through the alcove as Carter covered his face.

15

There was no escape. Everyone huddled inside.

The Rinder house on Jeff Davis Road shifted on its foundation, but didn't come down like the hotel and Spitz's house had. The boys' bikes lay scattered on the side lawn, out past the garage where they'd ditched them, but Ratman ignored those as he threw himself against the house. Glass shattered and the people inside screamed, but the house still stood. He pounded the roof with his rat-filled fists until thick blood oozed out of his skin, and the surviving rats inside him screamed in terror. The shingles split and the roof caved into the attic. Old toys and Christmas decorations scattered to the wind as Ratman clawed inside, but the house remained standing.

He staggered backward as the creatures that made up his skeleton struggled to stay together. His stretched skin sagged and bunched, making it harder for his servants to maintain their grip on each other.

He parted his lips and hundreds of red eyes stared out of his mouth. They each drew breath into their tiny lungs to give voice to his will. "Rinder ... Promise ... Retribution ..."

All six people inside the house heard the words, but did not understand them all. Tommy heard and understood his last name, clearly. He looked to his mother and saw his sisters hiding behind her, staining the tail of her shirt with their tears. His friends, Bobby and Spitz, looked as scared as his little sisters. He felt more terrified than they looked.

"Bring ... them ... out ..."

More windows crashed. Wood splintered and cracked from the front of the house and above. They gathered in the archway of doors, like for a tornado, watching cracks spread and widen in the ceiling. There was no storm outside, but some force of nature sought to end them, without remorse.

Silence followed. Not quite silence. The house popped and settled on its compromised supports, but there wasn't any pounding, and no unearthly voice breathing threats one word at a time.

There was movement in the other room. The boys pictured giant hands, reaching and searching for them through broken windows and broken doors. Mom recognized a sound like animals crawling.

Then, the first reptile turned the corner. It was a fat, pale crocodile, missing an eye and showing bloody, infected wounds along its side. Everyone screamed as Old Alice got stuck for a moment, too wide for the kitchen entrance. She snapped her jaws as drywall crumbled around her sides on both flanks.

Mom lifted the shotgun. All the kids clapped their hands over their ears and stopped screaming an instant before she blasted Old Alice in the face. The croc kept snapping with bloody flesh in ribbons around its skull.

Mom racked the gun as a lion staggered over the knotted back of the old reptile. It was wounded, too, but the shock of seeing the animal paused Tammy Rinder long enough to almost let it get too close.

She blew open the lion's skull, sending mane hair flying around the kitchen in bloody tufts. The beast looked so thin and fragile to Tommy, as it fell dead on the linoleum. The blind croc latched onto the dead lion in a senseless rage.

The shotgun was racked and fired again, in short order, ending Old Alice's suffering, as well.

More alligators slithered over one another as they came into view. They struggled and fought one another to climb over Alice's body, to fulfill their mission.

Mom scooped the shotgun shells from the kitchen counter into her pocket and grabbed up in one fist the two handguns she had set out by the sink when this all came down on her home and family.

"Out the back door. Everyone. Now!"

"Mom, that monster's out there."

"Gators in here," she said, "and the house is falling

down. Don't backtalk me. Go!"

They ran out across the backyard as the alligators and a malnourished tiger tried to follow.

Ratman leaned on the crumbling roof of the Rinder house, trying to keep his balance as the larger creatures were sent out to bring in the Rinder family.

Then he saw them running into the backyard. The mother, not really a Rinder, hid the two Rinder girls in a small shed in the back corner of the lot. He watched with his empty eyes as the Rinder boy argued with his mother. She shoved the Rinder boy, and two other boys of no interest to the Ratman, into the shed.

She stood her ground. She kept her promise. But she was in the way of what he needed to make his own broken promises right.

Where was the Rinder man?

"Bring … me … Rinder … boy."

Tommy heard those words from inside the darkness of the shed. He understood what they meant. He looked at the light coming in from the curled sheet metal at the bottom back of the shed.

Rats poured out of the Ratman's skin. Many of them dropped into the attic and worked their way down inside the house in the confusion of battle. Others knew their target and swarmed over the outside of the house, toward the backyard.

"I'm putting everyone in danger," Tommy said. "I need to go."

"What are you talking about?" Bobby whispered, as

if it mattered.

"He said my name. He wants me. If I stay, he'll kill my family and you guys. I need to try to lead him away," Tommy said.

Bobby whispered, "No." But he couldn't bring up anything more than that.

Spitz said nothing. He had heard the words, too. He didn't blame Tommy, or understand his plan, but he had heard the words.

Tommy rolled over to his belly and climbed out from behind the shed.

"Tommy, no," Ashley said, and reached for him.

"Don't go," Holly Anne said at her brother's back, but he was already gone.

Tommy looked at his mother's back one more time, as she stood in front of the shed. He never saw someone so brave in his life.

He also saw the dark shapes of countless rats racing through the grass toward her.

The Ratman ...

Tommy scaled the tall wooden fence and hit the ground running on the other side. Mom turned her head for just an instant, to see if something was coming up from behind her, but she saw nothing.

Turning her attention forward, she readied herself to blast shot at the field of rats, for all the good it was going to do. But before she could, the rats changed course, as if they were one mind, and they scurried up and over the fence.

Inside the shed, Bobby said, "We can't let him go out there alone. Not like this."

Spitz nodded in the dark. "He wouldn't let us go out there alone, would he?"

Mom breathed a sigh of relief until a brown bear barreled out of the back of the house, knocking the sliding glass door off its track. She held the shotgun down at her side as the last of the rats evacuated themselves into the side yard. She lifted one of the handguns and squeezed off calm shots, one after the other, as the bear closed the distance. All three shots struck its head and the third one brought the beast down a few feet shy of the shed. The dead animal's fur stank with an unhealthy filth that told her something more had been wrong with it.

The tiger exited the kitchen and trotted toward her with its tongue lolling out. Before she could raise one of her guns again, gunfire ripped from the neighbors' yards. The Jensons, next door, and the Coopers, whose backyard shared a fence with the Rinders, leaned over their fences with their rifles and gunned down the big cat. The animal staggered and then folded to its side under the onslaught.

She was about to thank them when the alligators poured out of the house and she joined them in opening fire again.

In all the commotion, Tammy Rinder missed Bobby King and Shawn Spitz climbing over the fence into the side yard.

With many of the rats out of him, Ratman slid, boneless, down in the driveway and started to lose consciousness. In that twilight state before rest, he sensed the Rinder boy traveling north, along Jeff Davis, with the bulk of the rats following him. The sensation was confusing because the boy seemed to be … keeping a promise.

A stronger sensation to the south broke the Ratman from any desire to rest.

The words danced through his alien mind.

Because we broke the promise …

He was still alive? Two Rinder men. Two broken promises.

Ratman forgot the boy and the two girls for the moment, even as their mother fought off animals by the shed and the rats continued to chase the boy in the other direction from the men.

"Return … to … me."

The few rats still in the house found their way out. The larger animals were no longer responding. He could not sense them any longer.

His skin started to retract a little, but not enough for him to stand with the animals he had within him. He crawled along the driveway and out into the road. It was more like a jellyfish trying to move across dry land, than it was a man using his arms and legs.

Ratman used everything he had to seize the barbed wire across the street from the Rinder house, a house that now stood crooked on its foundation. Cracked plumbing and septic already seeped out from under the place. After this day, the family wasn't going to live there anymore anyway.

With the fence down, Ratman said, "Fill … me."

The cows crossed the field and the entire herd shuffled into the monster's mouth, like returning to a barn.

He adjusted them around inside him as his skin undulated. The cows bit onto loose skin from the inside and pulled. The flesh drew tight enough around the animals inside for Ratman to stand twenty-five feet tall. With great contractions of rat and bovine muscle, the monster slogged south along Jeff Davis, toward the men who broke their promise.

16

Before the mob of prisoners returned from trying to break the security doors that locked Carter Rinder in as well, he slipped out of the alcove and down the stairs. On the lower level, there were windows with safety glass between the confinement area and admin. If he could get down there and get someone's attention, he could get out of here alive and whole.

The inside of his boot was slippery and greasy. And his foot was in agony by the time he reached the bottom of the stairs.

Carter lurched out from the stairs and held the walls as he limped up the dim hallway toward the wired glass enclosures. Even before he reached the doors, he could see the place was locked down, the lights were out, and the stations were unmanned.

He smoothed his mustache down several times in a row, trying to think.

Turning around, he found the hallway stood blocked by three figures.

Don't show these animals weakness.

"You made a big mistake coming down here." Carter brandished his club and stalked toward them, covering up his limp enough to make it look like a saunter.

Elroy Martin recoiled a step with the recent memory of his last beating, and with the swelling of his upper lip still fresh. The others didn't budge, one way or the other. When Carter drew close enough to see the one holding his father on a leather leash was Alias Orwell, he hesitated.

This was going to be a whole different sort of fight. Thoughts of being taken to California by a mob of vengeful inmates left his mind for the things he knew about this man who believed himself to be packed full of demons like rats in a grain sack.

His father looked like a shell of himself. He'd aged many more years than he'd spent in the Grinder. Hunched over, with swollen joints that quivered at the connections of rail-thin limbs, his skin sagged around his face and bones, like there wasn't enough of the old man left to fill it.

Elroy regained his courage in the lull and produced a filed piece of metal jammed into and taped to a piece of wood. "Look what I picked up off a dead Mexican, Rinder Junior. Should I use it on your daddy first, or you?"

"You should find your way away from me before I

finish the job I started yesterday," Carter said.

Elroy glanced at the side of Orwell's passive face and then back at Carter. "You ain't good at counting or figuring the odds, if that's what you think's about to happen here. Unless you're counting your bag-of-bones daddy."

Elroy poked Zell Rinder on the shoulder with his shank and brought a yelp from Carter's father. Carter shifted forward as he watched a spot of blood spread where Elroy had pricked the old man. Elroy's eyes widened in the dim light at the reaction from Carter. The disgraced doctor's smile pulled a little wider at the corners.

"How do you see this ending?" Carter asked. "I'm curious how your mind works, when you're clearly addled enough to think you got any power here."

The floor and ceiling rumbled. Orwell actually tilted his head up, but the others were occupied with each other.

"I got your daddy."

Carter shrugged. "Sure. Then, what?"

Elroy brought the point toward the side of Zell's neck. Carter's father tilted his head away, but didn't try to move his feet. The leather of the belt around his neck crinkled with the motion.

"Then, I kill him if you don't behave, Guard."

"I figured that," Carter said. "Might kill him on any account."

"You want him dead?" Elroy moved the shank by a

fraction.

Carter met eyes with his father as he paused before answering. "Don't know that it matters, but let's say you do. Then what keeps me from killing you in return?"

Elroy shifted his eyes to the side and then back on Carter. "You met my friend here?"

"We're familiar," Carter said. "He might kill me, but how does that save you, exactly, Dummy?"

"What?"

"What, as in, you didn't hear me, or what, as in, you're too stupid to get it? Speak up, inmate."

"What? I … No, you're not in charge here. You're outnumbered and you ain't strong enough to take us both."

"Didn't say I was gonna take you both, Dummy. I said, how does that save you?"

"What are you talking about?" In his frustration, Elroy's poker had drifted away from Carter's father.

Voices echoed down the hall from the direction of the stairs. A small quake traveled through the floor.

Alias Orwell turned his ear in the direction of the stairs behind him and his eyes away from the scene around him.

"If I don't care about stopping Orwell there, if it don't matter whether you decide to kill your hostage there, then nothing will stop me from ending you before I meet my end. You see now, Dummy?" Carter took a step.

Elroy brought the point back to bear on Zell's neck.

There were a series of thuds overhead and a large crash, with roars of voices muffled through the ceiling above them.

The end of the belt slid out of Orwell's hand and he turned his back on Carter.

Elroy said, "You haven't seen what I can do when I'm not chained down or locked away, boy."

Carter tilted his head. "You've seen what I can do when I'm bound by the rules, Baby Killer. Imagine what I'll get at doing when no one is looking."

That gave Elroy pause.

Alias Orwell turned his attention from the stairs behind them, back around in Carter's direction. Guard Rinder could have done without that, but this was his situation. They couldn't talk all day, he supposed. His feet hurt. One more than the other.

"I'll kill him if you try, boy."

"I'll consider that the starting gun on this little dance, Baby Killer." Carter adjusted his grip on his billy club where Elroy could see. It wasn't his first weapon of choice if he'd known the day was going to lead to this, but he knew Elroy was plenty scared of it, and that might give Carter the edge he needed.

A door crashed behind Carter, in the admin area. *Oh, thank God.*

"It's over," Carter said. "You let the hostage go and run along before you can't no more."

Another door back that way opened hard enough to vibrate the walls. They were coming fast and hard to rescue Carter. It was about time.

Orwell actually took a step backward. Elroy shook his head and cursed.

The impact behind Carter splintered and cracked the glass all around, but didn't break it free of the wiring. The next two impacts changed the shape of the barrier walls and shook the hallway intensely enough that Carter's vision blurred.

He turned too suddenly and put most of his weight on his bad leg, staggering him. He leaned against the cinderblock on one side as the indecipherable shape struck again. The vibration through the wall hurt his back. The security door bent in its frame far enough to see the shiny metal of the bolts within the twisted lock plates.

Carter's mind tried to turn the shape into a rhino or an elephant, because of the size of the figure crammed into the hallway, and all the loose, discolored skin hanging around its form.

"Uncle Sully?" Zell Rinder whispered, before he seized Elroy's hand and rammed the point of the shank, still within the doctor's grip, into Elroy's own throat, up underneath his jaw.

Elroy struggled, but weak and confused, as their hands turned greasy with his blood and Zell torqued and twisted the sharp point and edge around inside of Elroy.

Dr. Elroy Martin's knees gave out and Zell followed him to the floor. Zell felt it most in his knees, as he bent down on top of the man and stuck him several more times.

Orwell looked away from the Ratman ramming the door from the administrative side. He stared at Zell Rinder, with a guard's belt still around his neck, as he killed the other inmate from solitary. The voices had no comment on this, so Orwell didn't feel one way or the other about it.

After another moment, Alias Orwell turned away and strolled up the hall, toward the stairs. He was about to go up, but then the things within him, that he had tried so hard to fight for so many years before he got locked up, had something to say about it. He paused and thought on it long enough to be sure he understood, and then Orwell turned to the right, into a section of the prison he'd never been in before.

Zell tried to catch up on his breathing, as he used his faculties to straighten his knees up over the gory mess he'd made of Elroy. Lots of families around the state longed for the chance to do this thing themselves, but Zell had taken no real pleasure in it.

He turned slowly as Ratman pounded the security door out of alignment.

An odor reached Carter that swooned him. The whole prison stank, in a hundred different ways that Carter had learned to ignore. This brand of filth turned his stomach, but he couldn't tell if it was coming from a torn bowel in Elroy's body, or from the monster trying to break into the prison.

132

Zell left handprints on the wall and footprints along the floor, as he trailed blood past Carter, along the opposite wall of the hallway from where his son leaned. Zell continued toward the failing security barriers.

Carter reached for his father as the man hobbled past, but his foot threatened to give out on him and he had to lean against his own wall again.

Zell said, "Sully … Uncle Sully, it's me. Calm down and listen to me. I got locked up in here. The boy made a mistake. It was just a mistake. We'll make it right again."

Sully? The Ratman?

Carter couldn't wrap his brain around it all.

Ratman tried to squeeze one thick hand through the gap between the door and bulging frame. It wouldn't fit through. As the skin stretched and holes in the flesh widened, Carter saw the rats moving around underneath.

Carter stumbled backward and kicked Elroy's foot. The body shifted and more blood spilled out on the floor. Elroy coughed and bubbles rose up from his wounded chest. Carter cursed and left the wall behind, limping away from Elroy, who was still partially alive it seemed.

"Promises … broken."

Zell picked up the voice coming from the monster's hand.

"I know," Zell said. He leaned against the other side of the door. "I know, Sully, there's no excuse for it. I'm sorry. We'll do whatever it takes to make it right."

Carter limped a few steps farther away. *Speak for yourself, old man.*

"Pay … with … your … lives."

Zell sighed and looked over his shoulder at his son, slinking up the hallway. "I didn't do a good job communicating the danger of this curse, or the importance of the promise."

"Dad?" Carter paused.

"Broken … Promise."

"You make it right," Zell said, facing his son. "After I give him what he wants, make it right, Son."

Carter shook his head. "Dad? No."

Zell held his knees as he slid down the warped door to sit next to the large reaching hand. "It was my responsibility, Sully Rinder."

The voice breathed out from the hand itself. "Rinder …"

"You take your payment from me, you hear?" Zell said. "I'll pay the price for all. Take your revenge on me. Take me."

"Dad?!"

"Get the hell out of here while you still can, Dummy."

Ratman said, "Feed."

The rats poured out of the damaged hand and crawled over Zell, nearly covering him, before they started thrashing and tearing. Zell started to scream. A few rats wandered up the hall and others followed.

Carter nearly fell twice. He started to go for the

134

stairs, but then, looking up them, he knew he wouldn't make it. He limped down the same passage Orwell had gone, without realizing it. At his pace, the rats would have gotten him, except that they found Elroy first and opened his wounds wider. The disgraced doctor would have screamed, but the rats filled his lungs before he could. Elroy, in his dying confusion, pictured the souls of dead children tearing him apart from the inside.

As the rats returned to their king, they brought the bones from both dead inmates through the gap in the security door. Both had been promise breakers.

Alias Orwell, even at his easy pace, left out over a pile of rubble, through a hole in the side of the prison. He escaped well ahead of Guard Carter Rinder. He found downed fence out by Airport Road. From there, the ex-priest went east, all the way to the beach, and stared over the water for a while. As the tide came back in, he turned south and followed the coast for a while before he disappeared back into the world.

Carter had a harder time finding his way out, but he managed to circle around to staff parking and race north, toward home. His family had fled the house by then.

It was one of the Jasper kids next door who told him Tammy and the girls drove toward the beach, looking for Tommy, before the kid had a chance to tell her that he'd seen Tommy ride his bike north, toward the scrapyard with "all them mice a followin' him."

Carter thought about the Ratman and made his

choice as he drove away from the house, no Rinder would ever sleep in again.

Ratman strung up the bones along the prison fence, using the barbwire he'd dragged out from the fields on Jeff Davis. There was a lot of meat on the bones still, but he was in a hurry because there was more to do. Zell Rinder's eyeless head still hung from Guard Filmore's belt as the Ratman strung it up last.

The final few troubled and tumultuous years Warden Darren Hendricks spent overseeing the renovations of the partially functional Grinder State Prison, before it was fully reopened and renamed Robert G. Hucks Detention Center in 1984, he had a lot of time to think. He thought about why they kept him in charge during that awful interim after the storm and the riot, just to can him once the prison was rebranded. Him being in Myrtle Beach on family business during it all was a big part. Those bones on the fence, and especially the head, sort of sealed it. That and much more would be attributed to Alias Orwell's disappearance. No one wanted the job until all that history was swept away, so it was Hendricks' purgatory to manage before he was sent out to pasture as a failure.

Ratman finished hanging up the bones of the promise breakers and then the twenty foot monster moved up the road to finish his business with the Rinder boys.

jay Wilburn

17

Every time Tommy glanced over his shoulder, the rats were closer. His father had told him, at one point, that when you look back you slow down. Carter Rinder said it was true in running races, in football, and in everything. Tommy had asked why one time. Usually, his father bristled at questions like that. Tommy, when he was thinking clearly, stopped himself from asking questions like why. When he was really curious, he forgot and asked anyway.

That day, his dad had stared off in the distance, like it was actually a good question, like Dad might be wondering why himself. The answer Carter Rinder gave that day was, it might be lack of confidence. When you looked back to see where your opponent was, you were feeling afraid, discouraged, and you were thinking about losing instead of focusing ahead on winning. Another reason, Dad had said, was simple physics. You focus where you want to go, you give it all your strength, and you work into a stride. Turn your head over your shoulder and all that breaks down. Your muscles aren't aligned anymore, you're drifting sideways, and you're breaking stride because you're focused on what's behind you instead of what's ahead.

Hey, what are you doing back there? the patient asked.

Examination, the doctor grunted.

Then why are both your hands on my shoulders?

Tommy didn't remember where he'd heard the joke, and still didn't get it.

His thoughts were getting smudgy from exhaustion, waves of terror, and the surreal events of the day.

The rats were inside him … They are him …

He looked back again. They were closer.

"Rinder."

"Bring … him …"

The rats squeaked and whispered.

"Rinder."

"… back."

He faced forward, put his head down, and pumped his legs harder.

Neighbors stuck their heads out to see a biblical plague of rats and they slammed their doors again, without paying much mind to the boy on his bicycle trying to stay ahead of the rodent army.

As Tommy pedaled harder and harder, he thought there might be an exception to his father's rule they hadn't considered. When a person was running for his life, he might be capable of a lot more. Seeing the rats closing the distance behind him, motivated Tommy far more than it discouraged him. Hearing them speak could have driven him insane, if he'd had more time to think about it.

He hadn't really made a conscious choice to go for the scrapyard. It wasn't exactly a plan, as he led the rats away from his home and his family. He hadn't thought things through much beyond just getting away as fast as he could but, at some point, it just settled into his mind that that was where he was headed.

He didn't turn west when he got to the fences. The dirt path along the fence on that side was rough. He knew it like the back of his hand. The map spread out in his mind, from the holes in the fence, around the mazes of metal. He knew every rut and dent through the dirt. Tommy could have almost ridden it with his eyes closed, all the way to the breaks in the fence line.

But he'd never biked it with talking, cursed vermin, hungry for his blood, right on his wheels. The path was hilly and uneven. He knew he'd have to slow down, and that would be the end of him.

He continued along the pavement, pumping his legs until the pedals threatened to spin right out from under his feet. If that happened, he'd bark his shins and lose some edge on his speed, giving the rats all the opening they needed. He kept his feet on the pedals and spinning, as he drenched himself in sweat.

It didn't occur to Tommy to consider what he planned

to do if he arrived at the front gate of the scrapyard's official entrance and found it blocked or locked. There had been a storm, after all, not to mention the monster attacks this morning. It wasn't out of the realm of possibility that the yard wouldn't be open today.

But the gate was open wide and Mr. Lips leaned in the shadow along one wall of his shack, smoking. The cancer stick the man gripped between his thumb and forefingers was brown like a cigar, but thin like a cigarette. Tommy couldn't identify the brand, but something about the thin brown cigarette made Tommy think a woman should be smoking it, and not a burly, leathery, gnarly man like Mr. Lips.

Lips didn't know what to make of the boy pumping his bike hell to leather, like this kid was doing down the center of the street, with his head down like he wasn't even concerned about being plowed by traffic going the other way. Normally, he was quick to shout off any kids even coming near the scrapyard. They'd get themselves killed a hundred different ways in here, Mr. Finch would get sued by the parents and maybe the county, too, and Lips would get himself fired, with zero prospects for any other work. He would've completely understood Tommy's epiphany about being motivated by fighting for your life, if the two had ever had an opportunity to sit and chat as men.

With Tommy riding the way he was, Lips didn't even look around enough to see the rats. He also didn't consider for a moment that a kid riding with that level of sweaty abandon would consider riding past an adult standing guard. Never would have occurred to him.

Tommy made the turn hard and sharp, throwing sand and gravel with his sliding wheels. The debris peppered the gate posts, the wooden base of the shack, and the cuffs of the canvas dungarees Mr. Lips wore.

He shuffled his feet, like he was getting stung around the ankles, and put the cigarette in his mouth to free up his hands without thinking about it.

Tommy put his foot down inside the scrapyard to keep from spilling, but also to kick himself forward and keep from losing all his momentum. He was up and gone, between the first rows of scrap, before Lips could mumble out his first rebuke over the tobacco clenched in his teeth.

"Hey, you can't go in there, kid. Get back here." He was too surprised to even cuss, like he normally would.

The rats swarmed around his feet until the ground looked like it was made of them. He couldn't even see his boots anymore, as he remembered and used every curse word he had ever learned, in a string that sounded like a prayer meeting in the Holiness church up the road.

They started climbing his legs and Mr. Lips turned in three full circles, with his hands over his head, screaming a couple octaves above his normal speaking voice. They nipped at him, tearing his clothes and breaking the skin. He swatted at them, but they didn't respond to his attack, other than to draw blood from his fingers and thumbs. One bite hit bone and he swooned from it. Fear of falling down into them kept him conscious and standing.

They started jumping off the caretaker on their own, and continued their charge into the scrapyard. Not that getting bitten by rats was ever lucky, but he was fortunate that they had a much more specific set of instructions, this time, than to just feed.

He waded through them, to his shack, and slammed his forehead into the door hard enough to split himself open, under his hairline, at the front of his scalp. He kicked the last of the rats off his boots and they obliged, as they sensed he wasn't the one they were after, no matter how many promises he might have broken in his life.

Lips fell backward through the door and then kicked it closed in a panic. It was cloudy outside and not all that bright but, in comparison, he was in deep shadows in there. He scrambled to his feet fast enough that he felt lightheaded, as the blood struggled to catch up. He could hear the rats scratching the base of the walls as they scurried by outside. In that moment, he would have sworn he heard them whispering and speaking to one another.

He was sure they were inside with him, so, in a panic, he started to run. He hadn't picked up much speed when he slammed into a wall, but he hit hard enough that the old nails gave a screeching strain that sounded like more rats to him.

For a variety of reasons, Mr. Lips had his legs go out from under him and he drifted into unconsciousness on his back. His last thought, for the next couple hours, was that he was going to need more rat poison.

The rats finished entering the gate and spread out through the yard.

A moment later, Bobby and Spitz made the sliding turn through the gate. They raced past Mr. Lips in his shed, and chased the rats, as they tried to get to and help their friend.

The street was oddly quiet for a while, and then Carter Rinder drove by slowly. He considered the peaceful-looking scrapyard, but then kept driving. A little ways farther, he figured Tommy wouldn't have gone this far faster than he himself could drive it.

He turned around in someone's driveway. The old man rocking on the porch waved. Carter waved in return. Then he drove back to the scrapyard.

As he approached the gate, his attention focused through the chain link, looking for any sign of his son.

His chest jammed hard against the steering wheel, stealing his breath, as the car lifted off the ground and slammed back down on the wheels. An eighteen foot tall man, with loose skin and hollow eyes, dented the hood with one misshapen fist. Then, it threw another off-balance punch, grazing the windshield and lacing a crack through the glass, from one corner nearly to the other.

Carter bailed and slunk, low, around the trunk,

nearly dragging his bad leg at this point.

Ratman struggled to get around, as the running car kept pushing the giant along the street. He, too, slunk along the side and lumbered around the car as it continued to roll, unmanned, down the road, with the heavy driver's door still open.

By the time the Ratman stepped around the back bumper, Carter held onto the passenger's door handle and rode along toward the gate with the car.

"Broken … Promises." The Ratman struck the top of the fence, but then his skin hung up on the barbed wire and halted his pursuit. "Rinder!"

Carter staggered away from the car and through the gate, letting his vehicle go. He hobble-ran between the piles of metal debris.

The car drifted off the road eventually, and grazed along the last few feet of chain link. It ran up onto the dirt path Tommy had opted not to take because of the ruts, and it was those ruts that finally stopped the abandoned vehicle at the corner of the scrapyard property.

Ratman took hold of the barbed wire with both hands and ripped down long strands of it from the top of the fence. The ends snapped at rusted weak points as he brought it down and stalked after Carter Rinder, through the gate. He dragged the strands of wire through the gravel, sand, and rat droppings behind him.

Then, he sensed they were both here, the boys from

145

the last two generations of Rinders. He was close to finishing this.

18

Everywhere Tommy went, the rats emerged from the next row or the next turn, cutting him off. He turned and rode in another direction, too fast for this place with sharp, rusty edges and points. Then, the rats were there, too.

"Rinder."

"Broken."

"Broken."

"Broken."

"Promises!"

He circled deeper into the yard, knowing where he was, but feeling utterly lost at the same time. Then he had to backtrack, as the rats filled the spaces in front of him. Tommy knew he was heading right back into creatures hunting him, but he had nowhere else to go.

He stopped as the sun broke through the clouds for a moment. His head was already full of fire as he leaned over his handlebars. His skull throbbed with stabbing pain, and his tongue hung out like in a cartoon.

What's the difference between a man and his tongue?

She has some use for your tongue.

"I give up." He breathed the words out like a prayer.

I can't escape this.

Bobby shouted, "Tommy!"

He looked up and saw his friends.

"This way. Hurry!" Spitz waved, as if Tommy didn't understand which way he meant.

His legs were watery and his muscles felt full of lead as he tried to get his bike moving again.

"Ditch it and run," Bobby said.

Tommy did.

He still didn't feel like he was moving fast enough. His bike rattled behind him as the rats ran over the top of it. He found the energy to run faster. He refused to look back this time, as the passage between stacked cars narrowed.

Bobby and Spitz started running without him. Tommy wanted to yell out at them to wait, but he couldn't spare the breath.

He ran past the rotting body of a rat on the ground and then saw the open back of the house.

"Hurry!" Bobby yelled from the darkness inside.

The soft wooden boards absorbed a lot of Tommy's running energy and he could hear the rats' claws on the warped boards right behind him. This was where his life was going to end, he realized.

He sucked air and smelled something that reminded him of the heat from the vents at school in the winter.

Bobby grabbed Tommy by the shoulders and pulled him to the side.

Spitz held the flexible hose from their "experiment" with one old oven mitt. He struck a match with the other. A fireball erupted across the back of the house, and burning rats scattered into nooks and crannies between crushed cars outside. They tried to run from the fire on their fur and died as a result.

The rest of the rats kept coming, heedless, from their drive to obey their master. Spitz screamed as fire billowed out from the hose. He swept it back and forth, cooking the rats as fast as they could come at him.

He's going to die, Tommy thought, as he cowered from the intense heat in the hall behind the kitchen. The boards on the other side of the wall blackened and blistered. Blue flames licked up from between the boards.

Blue?

Rats squeezed in through holes in the front of the house, on the opposite side from where Spitz continued to burn them alive.

"… broken …"

"… promises …"

"They're coming in on this side," Bobby yelled.

Spitz turned around and washed flames over the walls of the house as he aimed through the hall.

"Look out!" Tommy grabbed Bobby's shoulder and

pulled him toward the back bedrooms, to keep from getting cooked along with the rats and walls.

They fell on the floor next to the dirty magazines as Spitz screamed in the other room. Smoke swirled around the ceiling and lowered toward them as the room filled up.

"We have to get out of here before we suffocate," Tommy said.

"We need to vent out the smoke." Bobby crawled on his stomach, like they'd been taught to in fire safety. Of course, fire safety probably also included the idea of not creating a flamethrower, using the old attachments in an abandoned house, in the middle of a scrapyard.

Those guest speakers from the firehouse never had to fight an army of rats before, though.

The wall splintered and a fat hand with rats' eyes staring out of the wounds reached in for them. It was smaller than before, but still giant. The boys backed into the smoke. The hand retracted and cars crashed outside as the stacks tipped over. The Ratman peeled the walls away as it fought its way inside.

The boys forgot fire safety and ran through the choking smoke.

Spitz dropped the smoldering oven mitt and kicked the charred bodies of rats as he rubbed his watering eyes. He walked into a wall and then turned back toward the fire in the kitchen.

Bobby and Tommy grabbed him. Spitz started fighting them, but Bobby said, "It's us. We need to get

151

out of here."

Fire licked across the ceiling above them, and then part of it collapsed between them and the front door.

"We'll have to go out the back," Tommy said, and started coughing.

They looked through the kitchen area, where the air wavered with the heat.

The sixteen foot tall Ratman stepped into view, between them and the outside. Its rat-filled fists flexed open and closed as it crouched and stared at them from empty sockets.

Six gunshots rang out and ripped through the body of the monster. The boys dropped to the hot floor when they heard the first one. Thick blood spewed from the Ratman's skin with the path of the bullets. A few dead rats and one bat fell from the wounds. Tommy swore he heard a cow moo.

The Ratman turned around and charged away from the burning house.

Tommy spied a figure at the far end of the row, hobbling away.

"Dad?"

All three boys started coughing and couldn't stop. The house grew hotter and darker, at the same time.

Tommy pulled on his friends. His throat was too dry to speak, but he did it anyway. "Go ... now."

He sounded a lot like the Ratman as they ran through the heat.

19

Carter Rinder climbed up the stairs of the crusher, and the Ratman followed behind him. Carter stepped off the platform and sidestepped out along the metal lip of the walls. The uncoordinated creature crawled up on top of the machine and reached across the expanse for him.

Carter wasn't feeling all that coordinated himself.

"Broken ... promise."

"To hell with that," Carter shouted. "I never promised anything to you. My daddy never promised anything to you. My boy made you no promise."

"Broken ..."

"You broke the promise, Sully. Or whatever you are now. You broke the promise."

Carter might have been imagining it, but he swore the Ratman paused. "Rinder ..."

"My father offered himself up for you. He paid the

price. You accepted his sacrifice, but you kept coming for us. You broke your promise."

"You … Rinder …" The Ratman crawled out further and Carter shuffled along, to stay out of reach. He wobbled on his bad leg, on top of the narrow walls of the crusher.

Ratman leaned out, opening and closing his fist, with barbed wire tangled around his dead fingers. "You … broke … the … promise … You … pay …"

"If I pay, does my boy live?"

"You … will … pay."

Carter raised his voice. "If I pay the price, you will set him free of the promise. That's the deal."

"Broken …" He crawled out further, but Carter had reached the corner of the crusher and had nowhere else to go but down.

"Say it's a deal, and I'll let you have me."

"Have … you … Rinder."

Carter raised the gun and fired the six fresh rounds he'd reloaded while he'd been arguing with the monster.

Ratman cried out with the squeals of dozens of rats. He lunged for Carter in a swell of rage, and fell into the crusher. Carter wobbled, but then shuffled back toward the platform. Fists thundered against the sides and Carter teetered, but kept going. A barbwire-wrapped hand missed him by inches. Carter kept going. Ratman reached again, but Carter leapt and tumbled onto the platform. He lost the gun and it dropped into the crusher with the monster.

The monster clawed at the smooth sides, but couldn't get out.

Carter climbed down the platform and reached into the controls. The key was in it. He turned on the power and then activated the lever. The motors hummed as the walls contracted on the abomination trapped inside.

"Consider that my promise to end this for good," Carter said. He climbed down and limped away.

Ratman tried to jump, but he couldn't get the remaining animals within him, along with their combined weight, to perform the trick. The walls closed in on him.

"Get … out."

He opened his maw and the herd of cows tumbled out. They shifted around in a panic within the crusher. More cows fell on top of the others.

His skin contracted, but not enough. He spread the rats out into his arms and climbed up the cows, as they struggled to get up themselves.

He caught a grip on the platform and the rats crawled over one another, inside his skin, to pull him up. With the other hand he lashed out with the barbed wire, over and over. The wire finally caught the lever and shut off the crusher.

He didn't know why it worked, and he didn't care. He just used the barbed wire to pull himself up and over. Then, he tumbled to the ground.

Carter turned down one of the rows of crushed cars, but looked back in time to see the Ratman running at him with his arms full, but his empty legs dragged behind him.

Carter showed his teeth as he tried to run, too.

Of all the strange things that happened that day, the one that baffled Mace Finch the most, was how all those perfectly healthy cows ended up in his half-closed crusher. Mr. Lips wasn't much help, with all his ranting about rats. How to get the cows out was an even tougher puzzle. All those cows in there … with a gun.

The boys heard six more shots as they lay on the ground, motionless. Tommy thought about his father, but then didn't know what to do to help. It took another few minutes for them to gain their feet again.

The house was smoking behind them, but not burning, and somehow it still stood. Flames licked up from the floor periodically, but the wood was too wet to keep burning.

They collected their bikes and started making their way around to one of the breaks in the fence.

Tommy fretted over his father. Was he supposed to try to help? Did his father want him to just leave, and let the adult handle it? He couldn't seem to get his frazzled thoughts together, so he just followed along with the other guys.

"What do you call a man with two wieners?" Bobby asked, as they barely pedaled fast enough to keep from falling over.

"Both y'all's moms' boyfriend," Spitz said and then coughed.

Bobby laughed a little, but it ended in a wheeze. He said, "Twice as busy and twice as disappointing."

"What do you call a woman with six boobs?" Spitz asked.

"A cow," Tommy said.

"Udder-ly amazing," Spitz said.

Tommy took a couple deep breaths and thought he could still feel the smoke in his lungs. "What did one saggy boob say to the other saggy boob?"

The Ratman dragged himself out into the gap in the fence in front of them. He was all arms and head. His body stretched out on the ground behind him, like some terrible serpent.

"Rinder …"

"Go!" Spitz said.

They turned their bikes around and tried to ride away as Ratman bounded forward on his arms, freed by not having all the weight to carry upright.

Spitz took in the most smoke while in the house, and couldn't draw enough air. Ratman caught up to him, but just knocked him aside.

"Tommy …" Spitz could barely whisper.

The Ratman caught up to Bobby. In that moment, Bobby leapt off his bike and swung the bike frame into the Ratman's twisted face. It gave a satisfying sound on impact, but the monster knocked the bike and Bobby aside.

Bobby lifted his head from the dirt. "Run, Tommy. Dump the bike and run."

Tommy let go of the bike and hoofed it. Ratman closed the distance, fast.

He turned a corner and Ratman struggled to pivot.

As Tommy weaved between and over fallen cars, the house came into view again. *God, I **am** going to die here.*

Tommy stretched out to try to grab the front door, still attached to the house, for all the good it was going to do.

The door swung open on its own and, despite everything, Tommy almost stopped in his tracks.

Carter grabbed his son and pulled him behind his body, shielding Tommy.

The Ratman charged them both, running on its hands, faster than it had moved in many years, but then there was an explosion. A massive propane tank blasted out from under the house and through the ceiling, where the boys' flamethrower experiment had followed the hose back to the forgotten tank that once fed the stove in a different life for this place. It ricocheted off two stacks of cars and then ripped through the Ratman's body like a rogue missile.

The burning tank flew out of sight like a rocket, then exploded in a mushroom of flame that topped the highest stacks in the yard.

Carter pulled his son around in front of him, as they stood in the dirt outside the ruined building, and hugged him. "Are you okay?"

"I don't know. I think so. Mom, and Ashley, and Holly Anne …"

"They're fine, Tommy. They went somewhere else, but neighbors say they're fine. We'll find them."

"Dad, it was full of rats." Tommy broke down crying and was sure his father would yell at him.

Dad said, "I know, but it's over now. I promised that I would end it, and it's over. We're safe. It's all …"

A rat climbed up on Carter Rinder's shoulder and tore through his cheek. More rats crawled around his body. Carter shoved his son inside the house and closed the door between them.

Tommy beat on the door and pulled, but couldn't get it open because his father held it. "Dad? Dad?! Dad!"

Outside, the charred and ruined skin of the Ratman inched forward between the cars, with the few rats still living inside.

A small voice squeaked, "Promise …"

Carter Rinder opened his pocketknife. "I made you a promise, didn't I?"

He clawed his way through rats and slashed at the crispy skin. Even as the rats tore into Carter, and burrowed their way inside him, he continued to cut at the monster's skin.

Inside the house, Tommy slid down the door in a heap on the dirty floor, coating his clothes in soot. He knew he needed to run, but he had no energy left. He lay there long after his father stopped screaming.

Then, there was a knock at the door. "Tommy?"

21

The door opened and both Bobby and Spitz stood there. They looked as exhausted as Tommy felt.

There were no rats, no Ratman, and his father was nowhere to be seen.

"My dad …"

Bobby and Spitz looked behind them, looked at each other, and then back at Tommy.

"You want to go home?" Bobby asked.

"Where's that monster?" Spitz asked.

Tommy took a few seconds to get to his feet. "I don't …"

The door slammed, closing Bobby and Spitz on the outside. A tight fist, full of squirming creatures, closed around Tommy's throat, lifted him off the ground, and slammed his back against the inside of the door, with his feet dangling above the sooty floor.

Bobby and Spitz beat against the outside of the door,

yelling for Tommy, but Tommy just stared in silent terror.

His father's face hung loose and limp, just inches from Tommy's own face. Beady red eyes stared out from Carter Rinder's lips and his empty eye sockets.

"Dad?" There was no breath behind it.

The rats breathed out their response from within his father's skin. "Promise … to … keep."

"I don't understand."

"You will … keep … the promise."

"How?" He could feel the rats inside his father's hands shifting against his throat.

"Come … to … feed."

"Feed? Where?"

"The … cabin … I … showed you."

"Dad? Are you in there?"

"Keep … the promise … or … your sisters …"

Tommy's eyes went wide. "I'll keep it. I'll keep the promise. I swear it! Don't hurt me. Don't hurt them. Just let me go, and I'll keep it. I promise."

The Ratman leaned closer and Tommy wished he was dead. He closed his eyes and waited for it to end.

"Remember … this."

The thing that used to be his father, the Ratman, released Tommy's throat, and the boy fell hard to his hands and knees on the floor that was still warm. Pieces from the fallen ceiling bit into his palms.

The monster opened the door, but Bobby and Spitz weren't there. The Ratman strolled out through the scrapyard, like he was going on a quiet walk in the country.

Bobby and Spitz came running through the smoking and blackened side of the house. They paused a moment to stare at the hole in the kitchen floor, and the missing section of roof over the ruins of the kitchen. They must have circled around when they couldn't get through the door. They ran the rest of the way to where Tommy huddled on the floor, heaving for breath.

They're good friends, Tommy thought.

They asked him over and over what had happened, but he wouldn't tell them. He didn't know how to tell them. After that day, they didn't talk about it much at all.

Tommy's mom would move Tommy and his sisters into an apartment in Fuller Beach after Carter Rinder was declared dead, and the house on Jeff Davis was condemned. Tommy ended up in a different school, and he drifted apart from Bobby King and Shawn Spitz.

Before Tommy knew any of that was going to happen, as he walked out of the house with his friends that day in July of 1979, he realized he had been right earlier. This was really where his life had ended.

jay Wilburn

22

Tommy Rinder wore plain clothes as he crossed the Ironheel Creek in the North Carolina parkland. It wasn't the exact same crossing his father had taken him through, over twenty years earlier. The river had evolved since then, but he'd used this particular ford and stepping stones a number of times before.

He pressed down the wide-brimmed hat that used to belong to his dad.

As he moved past the ruins and the graves, there weren't as many bone crosses or slaughter hanging from barbed wire as in the past. That wasn't necessarily a good thing. He stopped and stared at the broken well where his father had hurt his leg on their last campout together, in '79. He thought maybe some of those dark stains on the stone might be his father's old blood. Even their last memory together, before the Devil came looking for them, wasn't a pleasant one. Memories got smudgy out here, so he had trouble sorting the details.

Blood soaked in spots through the sack over his shoulder.

He started walking again and soon crossed the ridge to the cabin, beyond which looked much the same as the last time he'd been here.

Tommy stopped short and whistled.

There was no answer, at first.

He could just leave it, but over the years he decided it was better to be present and see that the promise was kept for certain before he left to return to the real world, where people ignored the smudges around the edges.

Unlike his ancestors, Tommy learned his lesson the first time.

The door kicked open from the inside. From the outside, Tommy smelled him before he saw him. Tommy walked up onto the warped porch and into the rancid darkness of the cabin, without further hesitation.

He unslung his sack and made to pour the contents on the floor. A cold hand closed over his forearm and stilled him. He could feel the rodents within the fingers, contorting to grip him with their bodies. Tommy mustered all his resolve to keep from recoiling or shivering in response as he waited.

"Give," the Ratman said, on the breath of dozens of rats.

Tommy handed the sack over and Ratman dug in, pulling the raw meat through his loose lips, where the ungodly entity sat upon the moldering bed. The rats, through rips in the skin, took their own shares from what dribbled down over the body that had once been his father. Almost all of the hair from his head and his mustache had fallen out.

The empty eyes stared at nothing as the monster fed, but Tommy felt certain they were looking at him.

He'd come up here every week since his father's skin became the vessel for the Ratman. As a kid, he'd used his father's dented car and had driven himself, every Friday after school, even when he was thirteen. His mother never stopped him, but never offered to drive him herself either.

He didn't have much of a social life, as a result. After high school, he'd dropped the idea of college. He'd moved up to a town just outside the park, to make it easier. He'd worked odd jobs. He became a park ranger for a while. That had helped. He'd refused transfer enough to where he'd been let go. He worked at a gas station for a while, but then became a deputy with the local sheriff's office.

Sheriff Greer had hired him, even though he had no experience beyond park ranging. She had taken a liking to him when he talked about his father working at Grinder, and dying in the '79 riot. She'd apparently visited the small memorial to the guards lost during that riot when she'd vacationed in Fuller Beach one year. She didn't tell him the story of Alan Hooker's bones, from back when she was a deputy, until he'd worked with her for a time and the killings had started again.

Somewhere along the way, he'd married a homely sort of local girl, who never wanted to leave town. That had helped. She couldn't seem to take pregnant, but when they had a son, finally, all Tommy could think about was the Ratman and the promise that was his family's curse.

His mother remarried after Tommy had gone to North Carolina, and Mom had moved to Florida with Tommy's sisters. He'd dropped out of touch with them as they went on to live ordinary lives, in a world where the rules weren't so smudgy.

Eventually, Tommy's wife grew tired of the town, but he refused to move, so she left him. She remarried, and Tommy's boy called some high school football coach in Virginia his daddy.

As Tommy watched the shell of his father feed, he wondered when he would tell his son about this promise. If he didn't, it would come to find him. His ex and Coach Daddy would not harken to the deadly madness Tommy tried to pass off as the truth, in these woods, for the Rinders.

"Hey," Tommy said, "how do you make your wife scream during sex?"

The creature made from his father's skin sat hunched over the bloody sack and fed, without responding.

Tommy said, "You call her and tell her about it."

The Ratman was bigger than last time. Maybe eight feet tall, if he stood up straight.

Tommy scanned the cabin and noticed the bloody clothes, strung on barbed wire along the back wall. There were a lot of missing persons reports in this area. None of the searches seemed to come across the cabin, or the village of Gomorrah. Tommy figured that couldn't be coincidence. Maybe it was in a spot smudged on the map, or in time and space.

Legends of the Ratman circulated like any other old favorite monster story. The incidents in July of 1979 were split between three explanations. A hurricane that no one could agree really happened, though the residents of Rutledge County, South Carolina swore by it, along with tornadoes that supposedly spawned, explained the bigger damage. The escaped animals from a zoo and reptile house explained other deaths and bloody bones. The law enforcement of the time didn't offer any counter-narratives, although many of them knew the truth. A serial killer, referred to as the Barbed Wire Killer, took up the rest. An old game warden, from '79 in these woods, was considered the first victim, but not the last. It got tied for a while to a person arrested in Ohio, but bones continued to show up in North Carolina after that, so it was still an active case. Some believed the Alias Orwell killings, that started up again after the Grinder riot, might explain the Barbed Wire Killer, too. That was an open question to everyone, except Tommy Rinder.

He wondered what would happen if anyone started questioning why Deputy Tommy Rinder found himself

172

wandering these woods alone, every weekend, for twenty years. If he ever got sent up for any of those crimes, well, prison wasn't a safe place to hide from the Ratman, was it, Grandpa? Then, he'd go after Tommy's son.

He also didn't know how much of Old Sully was still in that skin, and how much of his father made up that mind. Maybe it didn't matter.

"I keep the promise. Why are you still killing folks?"

"Mind … your … business."

That was his father.

"We almost got free, didn't we?" Tommy addressed the flesh as if it were his father still. "For just a moment, back there in '79, we almost had it beat."

The Ratman fed on, without giving an answer.

Tommy didn't know if that thought haunted what might be left of the man inside. It haunted the hell out of Tommy, and left him feeling hollow. His father had tried. He had fought for Tommy at the end.

"I keep the promise." Tommy turned to leave, expecting the Ratman to fall on him in anger or to breathe out the final order to feed.

He almost hoped for it.

Nothing came.

Tommy closed the door behind him and marched back along the ridge. He still had the whole day ahead of him. There would be a new set of missing persons reports waiting when he got back to work tomorrow.

They'd search, but no progress would be made on the cases.

Jay Wilburn

Jay Wilburn is a Spatterpunk Award nominated author with work in Best Horror of the Year volume 5. He has been a full-time author since early 2013 and you can see him write live on Twitch at *Twitch.tv/JayWilburn*. If you enjoyed this, check out Ruthless Rabid Raging Ravenous Rampaging Remoreseless Repulsive Revolting Repugnant Zombies! or check out his short fiction in Read Write Edit Play Repeat: The Select Short Fiction of Jay Wilburn Written Live on Stream volume 1. He also has more books with reasonable length titles.

More Books from
Madness Heart Press

Addicted to the Dead by Shane McKenzie
978-1-955745-15-4

All Men Are Trash by Gina Rinalli
978-1-7348937-3-1

Czech Extreme by Edward Lee
978-1-955745-06-2

Encyclopedia Sharksploitanica by Susan Snyder
978-1-955745-99-4

Extinction Peak by Lucas Mangum
979-8689548654

Mania – Revised Edition by Lucas Mangum
978-1087893983

Room 138 by Jay Wilburn & Armand Rosamilia
978-1-7348937-5-5

Trench Mouth by Christine Morgan
978-1-7348937-9-3

You Will Be Consumed by Nikolas Robinson
978-1-7348937-7-9

Made in United States
North Haven, CT
16 November 2022

26802785R00107